Going Too Far

I'm going to do my best to help Caroline with this, Chrissy resolved. *She needs a new boyfriend—she's been getting over Alex long enough. This new boy will be just the answer!*

Chrissy sat at her desk and took out a clean pad of paper. What could she say that would help Caroline? What advice could she give? She had seen Caroline around boys. She got the feeling that somehow her standard advice wouldn't be enough in this case.

I know, Chrissy thought. *I'll set them up in a situation that throws them together. I'll get Caroline together with her dream boy before she even knows what's going on. Maybe at a party . . .*

Other books in the **SUGAR & SPICE** series:

Janet Quin-Harkin's Sugar & Spice

Dear Cousin

IVY BOOKS • NEW YORK

Ivy Books
Published by Ballantine Books

Copyright © 1987 by Butterfield Press, Inc. & Janet Quin-Harkin

Produced by Butterfield Press, Inc.
133 Fifth Avenue
New York, New York 10003

Library of Congress Catalog Card Number: 87-90795

ISBN 0-8041-0038-1

Manufactured in the United States of America

First Edition: August 1987

DEAR COUSIN
Janet Quin-Harkin

Chapter 1

"Holy cow!" Chrissy Madden exclaimed loudly. The people around her turned to stare, and her friends exchanged knowing smiles. "Now that's what I call a fish."

She caught sight of the looks and grins and wondered what she'd done this time that was so funny. She glanced across at her cousin Caroline, who was still peering into the glass of the huge fish tank. Sometimes Caroline seemed embarrassed by Chrissy's exuberant behavior, but today she hadn't even looked up. *Maybe she's finally getting used to me and my weird ways*, Chrissy thought. *She's certainly not as uptight as she was when I arrived last summer.* She smiled to herself as she watched her cousin leaning gracefully against the glass, her ash-blonde hair still held neatly in its combs, while Chrissy's own straw-colored hair was blowing every which way in the strong January breeze coming in off San Francisco Bay.

Caroline turned away from the green depths of the tank to look at Chrissy. "That's where you'd be wrong," she said matter-of-factly. "A whale isn't a fish at all. It's a mammal."

Chrissy grinned at her. "How am I supposed to know stuff like that?" she asked. "It has fins and a tail and it swims. Don't forget the biggest underwater creature I've ever seen before this was a catfish my brother Jimmy caught. I haven't had too many opportunities to study whales in Iowa."

She leaned against the glass of the aquarium and peered into the murky water, where a huge black-and-white form could just be seen.

Alike and yet not alike, Chrissy thought, comparing the whale to her brother's catfish. Then she realized that this statement could also describe herself and Caroline. Kids at school sometimes asked them if they were sisters because they looked so much alike, with their blonde hair, blue eyes, and tall, slim bodies—but the similarity ended there. While Caroline was dainty and moved with grace, Chrissy sometimes felt she was a walking disaster. She was the sort of person who never walked if she could run, and she normally talked a lot to anyone who would listen. Caroline, on the other hand, was quiet and often kept to herself. She never yelled out when something excited or impressed her as Chrissy did.

And ever since Chrissy had come to California a few months ago, life had been crammed with new and exciting things—all of which made her yell out in delight.

The last two weeks had been the most exciting of all. She had been awfully upset about not being able to go home to Iowa for Christmas, but then Caroline's family had surprised her with a trip to Southern California. There they had done all the things Chrissy had only dreamed of before. They'd spent a glorious day at Disneyland and toured Universal Studios. They'd driven past the movie stars' houses in Beverly Hills (although they had seen only one gardener, who had waved a rake at them and told them to go away), and they'd seen the stars' footprints at Grauman's Chinese Theatre in Hollywood. What's more, they had stayed at hotels with swimming pools and health spas and eaten cotton candy while walking in shorts along the oceanfront—in the middle of winter! It had been a perfect vacation. Now that they were home, Chrissy's friends had taken her to Marine World, and she thought it was as exciting as anything they'd seen in Southern California.

Her friend Tracy linked her arm through Chrissy's as they moved away from the tank and down the broad, shrub-lined path. "You're going to love the whale show," Tracy told her.

"I've loved everything so far," Chrissy said. "It's so neat to be around animals again. I was so surprised when I found that they have all kinds of animals at Marine World besides just fish—and whales, of course. I mean, whales are adorable, but they are not cuddly like those cute tigers! They had such gorgeous smiles!"

Tracy giggled. "They were thinking about which one of us they wanted to eat for dinner."

"Well, what about those cute seals and dolphins and chimps," Chrissy said with a sigh of contentment. "They were all adorable."

Tracy grinned at her. "It's a lot of fun to come to Marine World with somebody who's never been here before. I've been coming here since I could walk, so it's all old hat to me."

"I can't get over having something like this right on our doorstep!" Chrissy exclaimed. "If I'd known that a paradise like this existed only thirty miles away, I'd have been here every weekend!"

Caroline laughed. "So you wouldn't have done any of the other things you've done since you arrived in California?" she asked. "Are you saying that the art fair and the school musical and the trip to Disneyland were all boring?"

"I'm not saying that at all," Chrissy objected hastily. "In fact, everything has been terrific, wonderful, and definitely exciting. What I wish is that they would rearrange the school week so we went to school on Wednesdays and maybe Thursdays and had the rest as a weekend. That way we'd have time to go to Disneyland and up to the snow and out to the ocean and over here every week!"

They passed an open area where goats and

baby llamas roamed freely, all trying to eat whatever they could snatch from passing humans. They paused, leaning over the fence to watch a little girl trying to wrestle her lunch bag from a goat. "That would be fun," Caroline said, "but then we'd fail all our exams, and never get accepted to college."

"Oh, Cara, you know I'm not serious," Chrissy replied. "I was just expressing my ultimate wish list. Besides, there are some fun things that actually look good on college applications—the school musical, for example. That was fantastic! I wish we could have another one."

"Unfortunately, they do only one production each year, and that's always in the fall," Caroline said. "There isn't too much happening this semester, I'm afraid."

"Will you two stop talking about school?" Maria broke into their discussion. "It is very depressing to think that we have to go back to school tomorrow."

"I'm so glad you guys decided to bring me here before school starts again," Chrissy said, beaming around at her group of friends. "It was really nice of you."

"We needed a final fling before the end of winter vacation," Maria said. "Don't you think it went much too fast?"

"It was over before it started," Justine agreed. "How come two weeks of school seems to go on forever and ever and two weeks of vacation is over in a blink?"

"Ours seemed to last a good long while," Chrissy said thoughtfully, "but that was because we crammed so much into it. All that driving, and then we were away nearly a whole week and we did something different every day. It was fantastic!"

"I'm dying to hear all about your famous trip," Tracy said.

"Yes, we want to know if Chrissy managed to bump into any stars besides Mickey Mouse. Did you really run right into him, Chrissy?" Maria asked with a chuckle.

"*He* ran into *me*," Chrissy corrected indignantly. "It wasn't my fault."

"So tell us, Cara," Justine said, winking at the others, "what else did Chrissy do?"

Caroline smiled sweetly. "Nothing at all. Don't forget that Chrissy is now totally used to our sophisticated life-style." Caroline paused, a twinkle gleaming in her eye. "Well, she did fling her arms around a total stranger in the haunted house!"

"I thought it was you!" Chrissy exclaimed. "I thought you were right beside me, so when the ghost scared me, I reached out for you."

"Oh, sure," Caroline said with a laugh. "I just find it interesting that out of all the people in the haunted house, you happened to throw your arms around a cute blond surfer!"

Chrissy felt herself blushing. Why did Caroline never think that Chrissy might be embarrassed over things, just because she was able to laugh them off? She still felt her toes squirming when she thought about looking up and finding that she was hanging on to a total stranger!

"And she did nearly the same thing when we were on the tram ride around the lot at Universal Studios," Caroline went on. "You know how they show you some of the special effects, like the collapsing bridge and the avalanche. Well, now they have a gigantic King Kong that comes up and attacks the tram. So Chrissy leans over to get away—right into the lap of the gorgeous guy sitting next to her."

"Well, this giant ape was only two inches from my face!" Chrissy tried to defend herself. "I didn't mean to fall into his lap."

"Way to go, Chrissy!" Maria said, patting her on the back. "That's a good way to meet guys."

Chrissy felt herself relax as she was swept along in this group of laughing, good-natured girls. They were teasing her the way they teased one another, and that was a good sign, wasn't it? At home her brothers had always teased her and she had teased right back, but here it was different. So many things were strange and new to her here that she sometimes didn't know when she was being ribbed or when to give it back. It was nice to feel that they now accepted her as one of them.

The girls walked to the top of a grassy hill overlooking the complex of show stages, animal cages, tanks, and lakes. Chrissy decided that Marine World was a perfect place—it was like a zoo and a circus and an aquarium and a picnic park all rolled into one. She gave a sigh of complete contentment. *Wait till I write to the folks at home about this*, she thought. *They will never believe me. They'll think I'm exaggerating again*.

As the girls reached the crest of the hill, the wind met them full in the face.

"Gee, it's windy today!" Justine exclaimed, fighting to keep her long hair from blowing across her face.

"Yeah, and cold, too," Maria agreed, pulling the zipper on her jacket higher under her chin.

Chrissy looked at both of them in amazement. "But it's January!" she exclaimed. "This weather is wonderful. The sun is shining and the temperature is way above freezing. What more could you want?"

Tracy nodded with understanding. "I suppose back in Iowa you have snow in January," she said.

"A few feet at least!" Chrissy replied, gazing out across the shimmering lake and trying to picture her house at home with snow as high as the windows. There were still flowers blooming here, and in Southern California a week ago she had stood under the palm trees wearing shorts. This whole world seemed no more real to her than a giant Disneyland.

"Do you think we should get our seats for the whale show?" Caroline asked. "I want to sit where I can see. I remembered to bring my camera this time."

"Yeah, let's get good seats," Chrissy said enthusiastically. "I want to sit in the very front row."

"No, Chrissy, that's not such a good idea," Tracy said earnestly. "I recommend sitting farther back."

"But I want to be as close to the whale as possible," Chrissy insisted.

"I don't advise it, Chrissy," Caroline joined in. "People in the front row do get a little wet, you know."

"Oh, I don't mind a little water," Chrissy said. "It will be fun! You guys sit farther back if you want to. I want to be where the action is!"

"No, Chrissy," Tracy said firmly. "Trust us. You'll get soaked."

"But I want to see the whale close up," Chrissy said. "I don't mind getting wet, honestly."

"You've no idea how wet, Chrissy," Caroline said kindly. "Come on, sit here beside me."

The girls slid into their seats about ten rows back from the tank. Chrissy sat beside them, torn between heeding their warning and wanting to be close to the killer whale. She could feel her heart beating fast with excitement at the thought of seeing a real whale almost near enough to touch. She had caught only glimpses of him through the green water of the tank, and he looked huge. Now he was actually going to come up to the surface! She glanced over at the others, all deep in conversation and not showing any interest in what was about to happen. They all took so much for granted, having grown up out in California. None of them really understood how exciting it was for Chrissy to see her first whale or her first ocean or her first palm tree.

"And now, ladies and gentlemen," the announcer's voice boomed out, "presenting Shamu, the Killer Whale!"

An enormous black creature glided from the far side of the pool. His sleek back cut through the water with tremendous speed, a small fountain of water spurting through the blowhole on top of his head. Chrissy leaned forward in her seat to get a better view. Suddenly the whale leaped from the water, so high that his smooth white belly surged into the air. Chrissy opened her mouth in amazement. The whale came down again and hit the water with a loud boom like a cannon shot. A solid sheet of water left the pool and headed straight for the bleachers, breaking over the crowd of children sitting in the front row. The kids were completely drenched from head to toe. All the audience laughed and clapped with delight.

"Now do you see why we stopped you?" Caroline whispered in Chrissy's ear.

Chrissy nodded, grinning. "I would have been soaked," she said. "Thanks for warning me. I had no idea we were talking about that much water."

"No, I don't suppose catfish make that big of a splash when they jump," Caroline said with a grin.

As the show went on, Chrissy became more and more entranced by the size and skill of the big animal. There was something about all animals that fascinated her, but this was the most impressive thing she had ever seen.

"Now Shamu would like to show you how friendly he is," the trainer went on. Shamu slid across the water and rested his giant head on the mat next to the pool.

"Who would like to give Shamu a kiss?"

A little boy from the front row volunteered. He put his face close to the huge whale's mouth. The audience clapped as the whale sank back into the pool, then reared up again.

"Anyone else?" the trainer asked.

Chrissy leaped from her seat. "Will you take a picture of me kissing the killer whale, Cara?" she squealed excitedly. "They'd just die at home if they saw it!"

Caroline grabbed her cousin's arm. "Hey! Wait a minute, Chrissy—you can't go down there. It's not—"

Chrissy shook herself free. "I want to do it, Cara. I don't care if it's not sophisticated, it's fun."

She started to run down toward the front row, praying that the trainer wouldn't pick somebody else first. But it seemed that he saw her coming.

"Ah, looks like we have ourselves another brave volunteer!" he called into the microphone.

Chrissy could feel her heart beating faster and faster. The whale seemed awfully big now that she was so close to him. His mouth was really huge, and all those teeth . . . She made herself think of the folks back home, passing around her picture. *Our Chrissy put her head inside a killer whale's mouth? I always said that girl had guts! She showed them what we're made of back in Iowa!* That's what the relatives would say.

She stepped up to the trainer and gave him her best friendly smile.

"Here's a pretty young lady to kiss you, Shamu!" the trainer shouted. "Okay, young lady, bend right down, and let Shamu kiss you."

Chrissy bent forward, close to the whale's gaping mouth, those sharp teeth. Suddenly she felt a shower of icy water drop on her head. She gasped, but no sound came out. Dimly she was aware of the audience laughing and clapping. She could feel the cold water running from her hair, soaking through her jeans, dripping into her shoes. *Chrissy Madden*, she thought, *how do you get yourself into these things?*

"You're a good sport, young lady," the trainer was saying, "and as a souvenir of your first kiss with Shamu, here's a picture we took of you."

He handed Chrissy an instant picture of Shamu spitting water from his giant mouth onto Chrissy's head. Boy, did she look silly! She managed to smile as she took the picture from the trainer's assistant.

"Let's hear a big hand for a brave young lady!" the trainer yelled into the microphone. Hands all around her were clapping. Chrissy pushed her sodden hair from her eyes and stared up at the crowded benches. Somehow the word *brave* made her feel better. At least she had dared to do it, even if she did look like a dummy. Nobody else had come forward, had they? She had shown her friends that she was willing to try anything once! *And I guess it must have been pretty funny to watch me*, she thought. *Well, I'll show them they don't breed wimps in Iowa!* With a broad grin, she held up the picture and waved to the crowd as she ran back up the steps to her friends.

But this is definitely one picture I will not send home, she thought, wiping a drop of water from the tip of her frozen nose.

"I've changed my mind about one thing!" she called to her friends as she approached them. "California is not warm in January! This water is freezing!"

Chapter 2

"Chrissy, are you mad at me?" Caroline asked in a small voice, as she and her cousin relaxed in their room that night.

Chrissy turned over in her bed and propped herself up to look at Caroline. "Mad at you? Why should I be?"

Caroline sat up in her own bed and drew her legs up into a tight little ball. "I thought maybe you were mad because I didn't stop you from getting soaked by the killer whale. I did try, you know."

"I know you did," Chrissy said. "It was my own silly fault. I was so determined to send home a photo of me being brave and doing something nobody in Danberry had ever done before . . ." She laughed, her cheeks turning pink. "But somehow I don't think I'm going to send home a photo of me getting an instant shower!"

"So you're not mad at me?"

"Oh, come on, Cara," Chrissy said. "You know me! It takes a lot more than a little squirt of water to shake me up. I'm the sort of person weird things always seem to happen to. You get used to it after sixteen years. I must admit, I was a little embarrassed at first, but . . ." Chrissy shrugged good-naturedly.

Caroline smiled at her. "You really are a good sport, Chrissy," she said. "I would have wanted to hide in the nearest bathroom until the day was over. I really admired the way you laughed it off and kept on going!" Caroline paused and looked closely at Chrissy. "But something must be worrying you, because you've lain there for over an hour and you haven't said a word. That must be a record for you—you're never quiet."

Chrissy lay back on her pillow. "I've just been thinking about things," she said.

"What kind of things?"

"About home, mostly," Chrissy said in a quiet voice. "I've been going through my folks' last letter . . ."

"Are you feeling homesick again?" Caroline asked gently. "Are you sorry you stayed here over the holidays?"

"Holy cow! No," Chrissy said firmly. "I wouldn't have missed a minute of that trip for the world. Disneyland and Universal Studios and Holly-wood—they were all places I'd only dreamed about, and they were even better than what I'd imagined. And staying in real hotels and eating fancy food . . . I had the best vacation, Cara."

"So did I," Caroline admitted. "It really was fun to have somebody else to share things with. I know I'd never have gone on the roller coasters at Disneyland without you. I even enjoyed the little-kid stuff like the Main Street parade and Alice's teacups."

"Alice's teacups?" Chrissy yelled, popping up in bed. "That was my favorite ride!" Then she grinned at Caroline and gave a big, contented sigh. "It was terrific," she said. "Every minute of it . . . and it was even better because I knew that they were having blizzards at home. Mom writes that they were snowed in for a whole week before the plow got around to our driveway. It seems hard to think about snow and winds that nearly knock you over when it's so mild and sunny here."

"Well, we have had an unusually good year so far," Caroline explained. "But the winter isn't over yet. We'll have plenty of rain soon."

"San Francisco's a wonderful city," Chrissy remarked, "but in spite of all the snow in Iowa, it is still a pretty terrific place. I just hope I can show it to you sometime. I'd really like you to see where I live."

"I'd like to come," Caroline said. "I'm dying to see you in action, trying to train your pet hog!"

Chrissy gave a big sigh. "I guess that's what I've been thinking about all evening," she said.

"Hogs?" Caroline asked, surprised.

"And cows and chickens and dogs and cats," she said. "Being at Marine World today, surrounded by all those wonderful animals, made me realize how much I miss having animals around me all the time."

"But I thought farmers couldn't afford to get sentimental about their livestock," Caroline said. "I thought you just saw them as things to be turned into cuts of meat!"

Chrissy's clear blue eyes opened very wide. "I am just nuts about animals," she said. "If you knew the trouble my family has with me! My mom had to drive me out of town at hog-slaughtering time, and every time we have to sell baby bull calves, I cry myself silly. And I adopt every runt piglet so I can rear it on a bottle. Why, I'm famous back in Danberry! Crazy Chrissy, they call me!" She laughed as she thought about it. "Then there's our dog and our cats. I never went for a walk without Bonnie beside me." She lay back staring up at the ceiling, as if she could see the dusty lane beside the cornfield, and the golden retriever bouncing along beside her.

"You've never talked about your animals much," Caroline said gently. "I didn't realize."

"I didn't realize either," Chrissy said. "But when I saw that sweet tiger, I just wanted to throw my arms around his neck." She lifted herself up and grinned sheepishly. "When I was about six or seven, I wanted to be a lion tamer. I begged my dad for a lion to practice on. I used to line up all the piglets and try to make them jump through hoops!"

Caroline laughed. "And did they?"

"Only when the hoops were between them and their feed bowl," she said. "But they were a poor substitute for lions. Bonnie was pretty good, though. I taught her all kinds of things. She's so smart." Chrissy reached across to her desk and picked up a crumpled piece of paper. "Listen to this," she said. "My mother wrote in her last letter all about the funny little things Bonnie and the cats have been doing. Jimmy got sent to bed because he was behaving badly at supper, and when my mom peeked in to say good-night later, Bonnie and the cats were all on his bed with him, as if they knew he was in the dog house and they wanted to cheer him up."

Caroline gazed thoughtfully at Chrissy. "I've never had a pet," she said. "My dad's allergic to animal fur, and I don't like slimy things like turtles or snakes. I guess I don't know much about animals."

"Oh, animals are the greatest," Chrissy said enthusiastically. "They are like best friends. They always seem to know how you are feeling. I can remember crying into Bonnie's fur so many times, and somehow she always made me feel so much better!"

"I used to snuggle my teddy until junior high school," Caroline confessed. "Sometimes I still do, if my day's been very bad."

Chrissy nodded. "That's why dogs are so special," she said. "When you snuggle Bonnie, she turns to give you a friendly lick, to tell you everything's going to be fine again." She paused, thinking. "Of course, she also wakes you up by jumping on your bed at five in the morning and licking you all over. Maybe a teddy wouldn't be such a bad idea!"

"You can borrow my teddy if it would make you feel better," Caroline said gently.

Chrissy sat up and looked across at her cousin. "Thanks, but I'd better not," she said. "I've got to learn to stand on my own two feet sometime, and this seems like a good opportunity. After all, I won't be allowed to have pets in college, and then when I'm out on my own it wouldn't be fair to have a dog or a cat and leave it alone all day."

"That's another reason why a pet wouldn't be such a good idea here," Caroline said thoughtfully. "Everyone in our family is always in and out of the apartment so much. My dad says that even if he wasn't allergic, a pet would just be a nuisance anyway. I suppose men don't get sentimental."

"Are you kidding!" Chrissy exclaimed. "You should see Ben! He is a big softie. You should hear him talk to his dogs." She cleared her throat and mimicked her boyfriend. "Who's a wovely wittle puppy then?" She lay back with a sigh, smiling at the memory.

"Ben sounds nice," Caroline said. "Are you still missing him a lot?"

Chrissy nodded. "He is nice and I am still

missing him lots and lots and lots," she admitted. "It's hard to be so far apart, especially after we've been going together for so long. You get used to having someone around to share things with and to go places with."

"Tell me about it!" Caroline said quietly. "I'm going through the same thing right now, remember?"

"I'm sorry, of course you are," Chrissy said. "Are you still missing Alex a lot? You haven't mentioned him all vacation. I'd hoped you would have gotten over him by now and be ready to go out boy-hunting this semester."

Caroline gave a sad little laugh. "Do I look like the type of person who goes out boy-hunting, Chrissy Madden?" she asked. "You know it takes all my courage to say 'Hi' to a boy without blushing. I don't know if I'll ever have another boyfriend."

"Sure you will. There are tons of cute guys in the school. Now you can take your pick."

"I'm not even sure that I want to take my pick, even if I dared," Caroline said hesitantly. "Right now nobody seems as right as Alex was."

Chrissy looked across at Caroline, leaning back against her headboard and gazing out with a faraway look in her eyes. *Poor Cara*, she thought. *It's been so hard for her. I only wish I could help her in some way, but I really don't know where girls like Caroline would go to meet new boys. It was all so simple at home—we were always getting together at someone's house after school and everybody just paired up. Things seem so complicated here. Why, sometimes I feel as if I need a note from the principal just to talk to a boy in the halls! But Caroline has got to get over Alex soon—it doesn't look as if he's coming back to her. At least I can give her some little nudges in the right direction.*

"I agree, Alex was a terrific guy," Chrissy said softly. "But he's moved on, Cara. It's no good dreaming about him, because he's got another girl now. Besides, high school romances are not meant to last too long, you know."

"What about you and Ben? You've been dating since kindergarten, haven't you?"

Chrissy laughed. "Almost," she said. "But it's different where I come from. If you move from one boyfriend to another, you are considered fast and fickle."

Caroline stared up at the ceiling. "I think I belong back in Iowa," she said. "It must be my Iowa genes coming out because I like your way best. I'd rather just stick to one boy . . . if he's the right one, of course."

"There will be a new, right boy coming along soon, believe me," Chrissy said kindly. "Just start school tomorrow with the promise to yourself that you are going to have a good time and forget that Alex even existed."

Caroline shook her head, smiling. "That will not be easy, especially because I'll be seeing him again every day, starting tomorrow." She looked across at Chrissy with a wry smile. "You know, it hadn't fully sunk in until now that we go back to school in the morning. Yuk! What a disgusting thought!"

Chrissy made a face and nodded in agreement. "Back to the brain factory," she said. "When I think about the amount of work your school piles on juniors, I sometimes wish I'd stayed home."

"Well, we have got the college aptitude tests coming up soon and your junior grades are the ones that go on your college applications."

Chrissy nodded thoughtfully. "It's really different here. Almost everyone I talk to takes it for granted that they'll go to college. That's not at all true at home. Anyone who walks around talking about colleges is labeled a grind. The cool thing is to get a job like crop-dusting or driving heavy farm equipment."

"Girls, too?" Caroline asked.

Chrissy scowled. "Girls are expected to stay home and marry farmers," she said.

Caroline looked horrified. "Surely not these days?" she asked. "That sounds like pioneer times."

Chrissy shrugged her shoulders. "Oh, some girls do go off to college and study business, or elementary education, but they usually come right back to marry the farmer next door."

"Is that what you think will happen to you?" Caroline asked. "Do you think you'll marry Ben someday?"

Chrissy flushed slightly. "It wouldn't be the worst thing in the world," she said. "Ben's very special. I like him a lot, but I know now that I've got to go to college before I decide anything. Mixing with all you career-minded people has made me decide that I have to plan a future for myself."

"So what's your plan?" Caroline asked. "Do you know yet?"

"I think I'll be a veterinarian," Chrissy said slowly. "That way people will pay me to fill my house with animals!"

"In which case you should be taking my biology class," Caroline said. "This is the term when we study animals after a very boring three months of plants. We are going to be dissecting all sorts of things."

Chrissy's eyes shot open. "You mean cutting up? Real animals?"

"Oh, not while they are alive," Caroline said with a smile. "I know it's disgusting, but that's the only way you really learn about them, by cutting them up."

"It seems too cruel," Chrissy said. "I did biology at my school last year, but there was no dissecting—except of flowers and vegetables. Mostly it was drawing diagrams of the reproductive systems of plants. I slept through most of it."

"And speaking of sleeping," Caroline said with a yawn, "I've just remembered that we have to get up for school tomorrow. No more lazing in bed until after nine. I'm turning the light out right now, so you'd better get moving if you don't want to undress in the dark."

A few minutes later, Chrissy snuggled down into her bed. From the other side of the room she could already hear Caroline's steady breathing. She lay there, staring into the darkness, and mentally prepared herself for another semester at Maxwell High. She would have to struggle to get B's and C's in her courses—especially math and chemistry. Life in a big-city school was so different from the easygoing life Chrissy recalled at Danberry High. Everyone out here pushed and shoved and continually rushed. It was fun at Maxwell and she could tell she was learning a lot, but city folk seemed to live under continuous pressure.

All except me, she thought, opening her eyes with a jerk as she remembered that there would be no play to look forward to this semester, nothing to keep her occupied after school. *I bet Cara and the rest of the group will all be rushing off in different directions and I'll be left with nothing to keep me occupied except chemistry homework!* she thought gloomily. In a way Chrissy felt sorry for the kids at Maxwell. They were always juggling jobs and sports teams and other activities with hours of homework after school. They rarely enjoyed the leisurely strolls home or just sitting around the kitchen table, sharing the day's events, which had been so much a part of her life back in Iowa.

"Home!" Chrissy mumbled the word to herself in the darkness. Every time she thought she had gotten over her homesickness, the thought would creep into the back of her head, reminding her that she would never fully break away from it. It would be cold at home right now. The windows in the mornings would be decorated with a lacy pattern of frost. Maybe the snow was higher than the windows again so that the downstairs rooms looked like an aquarium. Her thoughts drifted back to the animals at Marine World—to the killer whale and the tiger smiling at her and the baby chimp she had been allowed to hold for a moment. *Such sweet animals*, she thought. *If I had a pet to keep me company, I wouldn't mind so much having my afternoons to myself.* She patted her bed, remembering the familiar warm lump that was Bonnie on cold winter nights. *Poor Caroline, growing up with no animals*, she sympathized. *Maybe that's why she's so reserved. She's never had a dog or a cat to hug!*

Chrissy turned over, feeling the cold strangeness of the sheets. *I wish I'd taken Caroline up on her offer of the teddy bear*, she thought with a sleepy smile.

Chapter 3

"I can't believe vacation is over," Tracy said as she trudged up the hill beside Chrissy and Caroline. "Do you know how many school days we have before another holiday comes up?"

"It's only a little while until Martin Luther King Day," Caroline said with a laugh. "You can survive until then, can't you?"

"But that's only one day," Tracy said. "I'm talking vacation," Tracy said. "Weeks and weeks with nothing to do, no studying, no terrible SAT tests looming in our future."

"I'd say you have to wait until you are around twenty-two for that," Caroline said. "If you're not intending to go to graduate school, that is. Until then, every vacation is spoiled by worrying about what will happen next semester."

"Only a worrywart like you would spend your vacation thinking about the next semester," Chrissy chimed in. "The moment school is out I shut it from my mind until it starts again."

"Good philosophy, Chrissy," Tracy agreed, "but now it's starting again, and what a busy semester! It will be even worse than last—studying for the SAT's and the achievement tests, and going to extra coaching sessions for them, and the orchestra is entering a band contest—that will mean extra practices. I can't believe I'll have time to eat and sleep. It's a good thing the musical is over."

"I think it's sad," Chrissy said. "That was the most exciting thing I've done here. I don't know what I'm going to do without it. The evenings will seem so long."

"Then try out for something else," Caroline suggested brightly. "I'm going out for volleyball. I've always wanted to do a sport, but until now I spent all my time practicing ballet. I am so glad I finally realized there is more to life than jetés and pliés." She paused for a moment, then said, "Why don't you try out for volleyball, too?"

Chrissy looked doubtfully at Caroline. "I don't know a thing about volleyball. I've never played it in my life, except for that one time at the beach."

"There are other things to do besides volleyball," Tracy said. "What are the other spring sports, Cara?"

"Swim team," Caroline suggested.

Chrissy's eyes opened wide in horror. "You saw

my swimming ability when that giant wave swept me off my feet," she said. "What else is there besides sports?"

"There's always the chess club," Tracy said. "George and I go along to that sometimes."

"You've got to be kidding," Chrissy said, starting to laugh. "I can hardly sit still for five minutes. I'd never last through a few hours of chess."

"Well, what did you do at home after school?" Tracy asked.

"Cheerleading," Chrissy said. "But when I wasn't doing that, I never had time to be bored. On a farm you always have work to do with the animals. I used to be in charge of the hens, and any baby animals that needed extra attention—I used to hand-rear piglets that the sow over on Meyer's farm rejected."

"You see, Cara," Tracy said, her serious face failing to mask the twinkle in her dark eyes. "Chrissy is being deprived here. You should go out and get her a baby pig to keep her occupied after school!"

"If a baby pig comes into the house, the rest of us will leave," Caroline said, laughing.

Chrissy said nothing. While she vaguely heard the banter about baby pigs, she was concentrating on fighting back the big lump that was about to come into her throat. She hadn't missed her animals so much when she had been busy. First the art show and then the musical had occupied all her extra time and made her feel all bubbly inside. But now it was pretty clear from Caroline and Tracy's conversation that she was going to be the only one with nothing to do.

I mustn't be such an old gloomy gus, she thought, trying to snap herself back into a positive frame of mind, *but I do wish I had a pet to care for here. That would solve everything.*

"So tell us about the piglets," Tracy urged Chrissy. "Did you really house-train them, like you once told Dolores? Or did they run around with cute little diapers on?"

"I really don't want to talk about it now," Chrissy said quietly. "It only makes me upset to think about my animals."

"Chrissy's suffering from animal withdrawal symptoms," Caroline told Tracy. "Being at Marine World reminded her of all the animals she left behind."

"I thought farmers considered all animals as potential hamburgers," Tracy said, giving Chrissy a wicked grin. Chrissy tried to return it with a withering stare that made Tracy giggle.

"I happen to be wild about animals," she said, then also started to giggle as she realized what she'd said.

"I can second that statement," Caroline said firmly. "First she kept me awake last night reminiscing about every pet she'd ever had, and she's been oohing and aahing over every animal we've met all morning."

"I have not," Chrissy said. "There just seems to be a lot of cute animals out today, and I'm remarking on that fact. You have to admit that the little kitten we saw perched on the fence was adorable."

"So why don't you get a pet of some sort, if you're missing them so much?" Tracy suggested. "I'm sure Caroline's folks wouldn't mind."

"I'm not so sure," Caroline said hesitantly. "My dad's allergic to animal hair."

"I wasn't suggesting a dog or a cat," Tracy said. "There are plenty of other things. A hamster or a gerbil."

Caroline gave a horrified laugh. "They all have hair, Tracy! Besides, you don't know my father! He'd freak out if he saw a little furry thing scurrying across his floor. He just doesn't like animals."

"Well, maybe not furry, then," Tracy went on.

"And don't suggest a reptile," Caroline said, "because my mother freaks out if she sees a snake or a lizard—and I'm not too wild about them either!"

"It's okay, Tracy," Chrissy said. "I'm sure I can survive without my animals for a few more months. I wouldn't want to upset Caroline's family. I'm sure I'll find something to do with myself to keep busy."

As Chrissy looked down at the sidewalk, something near the street moved.

"Oh, look at that poor little pigeon!" she exclaimed, her unhappiness forgotten for the moment. "It looks like it's hurt its wing! What should we do?"

"Chrissy!" Caroline said, grabbing her cousin's arm as she ran toward it. "It's only a pigeon. Don't touch it. They carry disease."

"But it might be hurt!" Chrissy exclaimed. She reached for the pigeon, which flapped into the air and flew off to the nearest house top as Caroline and Tracy laughed.

"You are funny!" Tracy said. "Chrissy Madden's save-the-pigeon society!"

"It might have been hurt!" Chrissy said. "And it was so sweet. All soft and fluffy."

"This city has too many pigeons. Most people want to get rid of them," Caroline pointed out.

"Well, I like pigeons," Chrissy declared.

"You'd better watch her, or you might wake up one morning with a sweet little pigeon cooing on your pillow," Tracy said to Caroline with a playful nudge.

"Mama mia, Chrissy!" Caroline said, throwing up her hands in a characteristic gesture of exasperation. "You've really got it bad . . . wanting to adopt an injured pigeon!"

Chrissy smiled, going along with the teasing, even though it still made her uneasy. "I don't see what's so strange about liking animals or wanting a pet," she said. "After all, most people keep pets. Even in the city you see dogs on leashes all the time."

"Yes, for heaven's sake, Caroline, get the poor girl a pet!" Tracy interjected.

"Perhaps we'd better get you a pet, Chrissy, before you come home with wounded pigeons or stray cats," Caroline said. "I don't suppose my family would object to something like a goldfish."

Chrissy's eyes lit up. "I wouldn't mind settling for a goldfish," she said. "They are so cute, the way they stare at you through the glass with those big eyes."

The other two girls laughed as they walked up the steps into the main entrance of the high school.

At lunch Chrissy and Caroline met their friends, as usual, at the little park up on the hill. Tracy was there, and Justine with her boyfriend, Randy, and Maria with her boyfriend, Dino. Only Alex was missing from the picture. Chrissy glanced across at Caroline, wondering if she was also thinking about Alex right now.

Poor Cara, she thought. *He was such a nice boyfriend for her. She's so shy—I wonder if she'll meet anyone as nice as Alex.* Chrissy looked around the park, remembering the times Alex had been there with them. He had always had time to talk to her when she had a big problem. In fact, he had been a special friend to her, too. And now he was off with Jan Blackman, who was nice, but not as nice as Cara. The world was definitely an unfair place. *I'll have to help Cara find a new boyfriend, she decided, taking a large bite from her sandwich. She certainly needs a gentle push from somebody! She's so shy that she'd never dare go up to a guy she likes. I wonder how she ever dared talk to Alex.*

"So what are our priorities this quarter?" Randy asked the group. "Do we have any parks to save, or can we relax and attack our five hours of homework every night?"

"Our number-one priority is to find Chrissy a goldfish!" Tracy said with a giggle.

"*A what?*" Chrissy grinned sheepishly at the puzzled faces of her friends.

"She needs a pet to keep her occupied in the afternoons, and she's pining away for her animals at home," Tracy went on. "In fact, it's getting so serious that she's about to start adopting stray sea gulls!"

Chrissy looked in horror at the huge white birds, perched today as every day, on benches just out of reach, waiting to swoop in and steal food. With their red eyes and fierce beaks, they still looked frightening to Chrissy. She could remember, all too clearly, the time one had stolen her sandwich and Alex had come to rescue her. "Not sea gulls," she said. "I still haven't forgotten that time when one stole my lunch right out of my hands and would have flown off with it, but A—" She broke off, realizing how tactless it would be to talk about Alex right now. "Anything but sea gulls," she said firmly.

"So you've decided to settle for a goldfish instead?" Randy asked seriously. "Good idea. Then we can always come to you if we decide to have a goldfish-eating contest!"

"Randy, you are the world's most terrible tease," Justine said, noting Chrissy's wide-eyed look of horror. "Don't you listen to him, Chrissy. I think goldfish are a great idea—they don't need to go for walks, they don't mess up the carpet, and they don't bark to be let out."

"Can we all come and help choose?" Maria asked. "It's very important to get a fish with the right personality."

"Hey! Wait a minute," Justine said, rummaging in her bag. "I'm sure there was an ad for fish in the school newspaper that came out this morning. I remember noticing something about aquariums. Maybe you can pick up a good bargain." She began to browse through the weekly paper, with Caroline and Tracy peering over her shoulder. Chrissy waited patiently, thinking secretly that anything that called itself an aquarium was going to be too expensive for her. What she had in mind was a bowl from Woolworth's, a bit of seaweed, and one fish.

"Here's the want ads," Tracy said, leaning over Justine's shoulder to point at the page. "Harley Davidson . . . Hey! How about a motorcycle instead of a fish, Chrissy?"

"Here it is—aquarium for sale," Justine read out triumphantly. "It says 'Aquarium, salt water, one hundred gallons . . . ' Oh, no!"

She started to laugh. Tracy and Caroline started to laugh, too.

". . . and fully stocked with piranhas!" Tracy finished off. "It must be another of their joke ads. Boy, those guys on the newspaper staff are beginning to bug me. Why can't they take anything seriously?"

"I think they are pretty funny," Dino said. "Did you see their new Aunt Fanny column? It was great." He leaned across and took the paper from them. "Listen to this one, guys: 'Dear Aunt Fanny, I have this big problem. When I'm depressed I can't seem to stop eating pizza! Signed, Fat Cat.' And Aunt Fanny's answer is: 'There is an easy cure for your problem, dear Fat Cat. Next time you get a craving for pizza, try lasagna instead!'"

The group broke into noisy laughter. Chrissy looked from one person to the next, wondering what was so funny about Dear Aunt Fanny. It sounded to her that Fat Cat might have a real problem. Sometimes Chrissy couldn't understand city humor, and she wasn't sure she ever wanted to. She opened her mouth to speak, hesitated, then spoke anyway. "I don't think that's very funny, you guys," she said.

The rest of the group abruptly stopped laughing.

"Oh, Chrissy, where's your sense of humor?" Justine asked. "It's just a takeoff on those dreadful Dear Abby-type of columns."

"But what if it isn't just a takeoff?" Chrissy asked. "I mean, supposing a real person wrote in to Dear Aunt Fanny? Think how she'd feel if she had that problem and then she saw that people were laughing at her."

"I don't think they have real people writing in," Justine said uneasily. "I think they just make up the questions."

"But if someone had that problem, they'd still feel bad," Chrissy said. "I think it's a bad idea to make fun of problems, because everybody's got at least one."

"Chrissy Madden, not only champion of animals' rights, but also of people's rights!" Justine said.

Chrissy looked from one laughing face to the next. They obviously all thought she was acting like a weirdo again. They were always putting one another down with their own jokes. In fact, humor in the city seemed to consist entirely of scoring off other people with one-liners, just like on TV shows. Chrissy didn't usually admit that she found these kinds of jokes in poor taste, but she felt she had to stand up for herself today, however weird they thought she was.

"Just think about when you've had problems," she said, feeling the heat creeping into her face. "How would you feel if you opened the newspaper and there was your problem with a real put-down answer beside it. You'd feel that nobody took your problem seriously except you! Those guys at the newspaper should realize they have a responsibility."

"You tell 'em, Chrissy!" Randy said, stretching languidly on the arm of the park bench. "In fact, why don't you go down and see the editor and tell him to shape up!"

"That's a good idea. I think I will," Chrissy said, jumping up from her seat. "Where is the newspaper office?"

"Down in the basement somewhere," Caroline said, looking at her cousin with concern, "although I don't think they'd be there right now. I think they usually meet after school." She put her hand on Chrissy's arm. "Are you sure you want to do this, Chrissy? Those guys down at the *Clarion* have a reputation for having a wicked sense of humor. I don't want you to be the target of their next jokes. Why don't you forget it? After all, it's only a little school newspaper and a few guys having fun."

"I know," Chrissy said, "and maybe I am making a big thing out of nothing. But I keep thinking about home. Everyone always goes to my Grandma Madden for advice when they have a problem. She's the local Aunt Fanny and she's proud of it. There are some pretty weird and funny problems, even where I come from, but Granny Madden never betrays a confidence or makes fun of anyone. I just don't think you should have a column like this if you're not going to offer real help to people—and I'm going to tell the editor that."

She could feel her cheeks burning bright red as she spoke. She knew she was not acting like a cool city girl, but like a naïve girl fresh from the country. Maybe the sophisticated kids at school would only laugh at the column. Maybe nobody would ever think of taking it seriously . . . but just suppose one day one person felt that nobody cared, because he or she read a slick answer like that? Wasn't it worth looking like a fool for what one believed in? That's what her parents had always brought her up to believe.

Chrissy wanted very much to be cool and sophisticated like Caroline and her friends—*but there are some things in life you have to take seriously*, she decided, *and helping other people is one of them!*

Chapter 4

Maxwell High was an old building, built before the great earthquake of 1906. As Chrissy descended the stone steps to the basement that afternoon, she couldn't help feeling that nobody had altered the building since that date. The basement hallway was dark and creepy, with a vaulted ceiling and narrow archways. The arches threw pools of black shadows between the lights. After the doors leading to the wood and metal shops, the hallway turned a corner, where it was lit by a single, naked light bulb. Chrissy went forward cautiously, feeling more and more with every step that she was playing out a scene in a horror movie. She had seen lots of horror movies in which the heroine went down into the dungeons of the castle, along a darkened, vaulted hall, and was finally grabbed by a scary monster or giant earthworm!

She had almost decided to turn back when she heard the friendly clatter of a typewriter coming from behind the last door. A sheet of paper tacked to the door read: SILENCE, YOU ARE IN THE PRESENCE OF A GENIUS AT WORK. Timidly, she tapped on the door. When nobody answered, she let herself into the room.

The typist, a large boy with unruly brown curls, stopped his work and looked up. He was hardly the type of person Chrissy had expected to meet in the newspaper office. In fact, he looked as if he would be more at home on the football field than behind a tiny desk in an office hardly bigger than a closet.

"Hi, there," he said, looking at her curiously. "I assume you've come to see me, since nobody ever wanders down here by accident." He paused and studied her from head to toe. "You seem familiar—do I know you?"

"I'm Chrissy Madden," Chrissy began hesitantly, taking in the incredible clutter that covered every surface, "and I don't know if I've come to the right place, but I'd like to talk to Aunt Fanny."

"You what?" The boy looked puzzled.

"Aunt Fanny," Chrissy repeated. "You know . . . Dear Aunt Fanny in the newspaper? This is the *Clarion* office, isn't it? I want to know how to get in touch with Aunt Fanny."

A slow smile spread across the broad face. "You

want to talk to Aunt Fanny?"

"That's right. I have a complaint about the way this column is being written, and I'd like to talk to Aunt Fanny about it."

"A complaint, huh? Sounds serious. Are you one of those censorship people? I don't think there was too much sex and violence in Aunt Fanny this week, was there?"

Chrissy shifted uneasily from foot to foot under his mocking gaze.

"I'd rather just discuss it with Aunt Fanny," she said primly. "Would you please let me know how I can get in touch with her?"

The boy's smile broadened. "You're talking to her," he said. "Now, what was your problem?"

Chrissy opened her mouth, but no words would come. Earlier, when she had thought out what she would say when she met Aunt Fanny, she had not, for one moment, imagined that Aunt Fanny would turn out to be a hefty six-foot-tall boy!

"You're putting me on," she managed to say at last.

The boy shook his head easily. "Trust me," he said. "I am Aunt Fanny, only don't let it get around. My fans would be devastated."

"Oh, but I thought . . ." Chrissy began to stammer.

The boy chuckled. "Don't tell me you expected to see a lovely gray-haired old lady sitting here doing her knitting? Somehow I don't think you'll find too many of those around high school. They kick you out if you haven't graduated in fifty years!"

Chrissy was very conscious of his sarcastic smile and his cool eyes, flecked with brown like a tiger's. She could just see him recounting this story to his friends and everyone laughing at her. Her rising anger took away any hesitancy she might have had.

"Well, I might have guessed that a boy would have written the column," she said. "Any girl would have been more sensitive!"

"To what?"

"Your answers—they were all just making fun of people. They weren't real answers at all!"

"But they weren't real questions," the boy said, still looking amused. "We needed something to fill half a column a couple of issues ago, and somebody suggested doing Dear Aunt Fanny for a joke. We just kept it in because kids thought it was funny."

"Well, I don't," Chrissy said.

"I can tell that," the boy replied. "But then not everybody is blessed with a sense of humor."

"I have a perfectly good sense of humor," Chrissy said firmly, "but I think it is very dangerous to turn problems into humor. Have you ever thought how you would feel if one of your readers had the problem you featured in your column, and saw your funny answer? It would make the person feel even more depressed."

The boy's face suddenly grew serious. "I hadn't thought of that," he said. Then the smile reappeared. "Oh, but, come on. I mean, nobody is going to take the column seriously, are they?"

"I would, if I read about my problem," Chrissy said.

"And what is your problem?" he asked, raising an eyebrow suggestively.

"Right now I'm trying to get it through the head of a stubborn boy that he is playing with fire!" Chrissy answered.

The boy threw back his head and laughed. "I know who you are now," he said. "I thought I met you before. We did an article on you when you hijacked a bulldozer to save the park. You must be a dangerous person! Do you spend your entire life stirring things up?"

"Only when I feel something is worth fighting for," Chrissy said.

The boy looked at her steadily. "I'm flattered that you think our newspaper is worth fighting about. I sometimes think that all it's used for is cat litter boxes and paper airplanes."

"I just feel," Chrissy said slowly, "that there is plenty of room in a newspaper for humor, but not in a column that could be of genuine help to people. Who has more problems than high school kids? We all have worries, and lots of us have nobody to discuss them with. A real question-and-answer column might help a lot of people, if you gave caring, common-sense answers."

The boy leaned back in his chair and looked hard at Chrissy. "You want the job?" he asked.

"The job?"

"Yeah—if you think the column might be a good idea, we'll try it. You're hired. You write the answers, since you obviously care enough about other people to come down here and start attacking me. I need one column per week—think you can handle that?"

"But I've never tried writing for a newspaper before," Chrissy said hesitantly. "I mean, I wouldn't know where to begin. . . ."

"So . . . none of us is an expert," the boy said, already starting to rearrange the mountain of papers on his desk in what Chrissy guessed to be an effort to look cool and efficient. "We all started out here as cub reporters. I had to work my way up to editor, picking up skills along the way until I became the slick newspaperman I am now. . . ."

As he spoke, the mountain tottered and fell to the floor, creating an avalanche of papers scattering in all directions. Before she could stop herself, Chrissy burst out laughing.

"I think I will take the job," she said, picking up the papers. "I get the feeling a slick newspaperman like you might need some help! You can always write to Dear Aunt Fanny about your problem, you know!"

She looked up and smiled sweetly. The boy smiled back, although she could tell that he was not too happy with her.

"Do you have a name—besides Aunt Fanny, I mean?" she asked, dumping a huge pile of papers back on his desk.

"It's Jay," he said, not taking his tiger-flecked eyes off her for a second. "Jay Kramer."

"Nice to meet you, Jay Kramer," Chrissy said, giving him a broad smile. "I'm looking forward to working with you."

"I'm not sure that I can say the same," Jay said, returning a half smile. "I have a feeling I've just let myself in for a lot of trouble."

"Trouble? What do you mean?" Chrissy asked innocently.

"You!" Jay said. "So remember, Aunt Fanny— only on a trial basis. We'll give it a couple of issues, and if it doesn't catch on, we'll take it out again."

Chapter 5

Chrissy walked home in a thoughtful mood. Now that she was out of Jay's office, she was filled with second thoughts. *What do you know about giving advice?* she asked herself severely. *Your folks would die laughing if they knew you were acting as Aunt Fanny. They'd tell you that you could never even sort out your own problems without going into a flat-out panic each time!*

She imagined Ben's reaction. *You—Aunt Fanny?* he would ask, his blue eyes creasing at the sides as he tried to hide a smile. *And what do you know about the big bad world, girl?*

Ben, she thought with a sigh. *You are so far away . . . and maybe you are right. What do I know about this strange world in San Francisco where people like Jay make a joke out of every-*

thing?

She thought about Jay and his mocking smile. *I can't back down now*, she decided. *Or he will think I'm a coward. Besides, I really might be able to help people. There are so many kids at this school from one-parent families or even have two parents who don't give them the time of day. And there must be tons of kids who feel like nobody understands them. Maybe they'd like to have the chance to discuss a problem with some-one they don't know. Gee, wouldn't it be great if the column was a hit and it became the most popular thing in the newspaper? I can just see Jay's face if that happened. Pity I can't tell anyone who Aunt Fanny really is.*

Keeping Aunt Fanny's identity a secret was something Jay had insisted on, and Chrissy had to agree it was a good idea.

"If people know who they are writing to, they'll think twice about writing," Jay had suggested. "But if they believe there really is a mythical Aunt Fanny out there, then they'll all want to spill out their problems. I hope we get some good, juicy ones," he had finished, giving Chrissy a wink, followed by a grin that showed he knew he was annoying her.

That guy really thinks a lot of himself, Chrissy thought. *But I won't have to work with him too much, just hand in my column. . . .*

She climbed the steps to Caroline's apartment, wishing again that she could share her secret with her cousin. It was going to be hard keeping something from Cara when they shared so much, but she had promised Jay she wouldn't tell anyone—and that included Caroline.

"Is that you, Chrissy?" Caroline called down the hall as soon as Chrissy had walked through the door. "Where have you been? I've been waiting and waiting for you to come home!"

Caroline's head poked out from the bedroom door.

"I went to see the newspaper guy," Chrissy said.

Caroline's eyes opened wide. "You really went? You're brave. I don't think I'd dare go down in that basement to a den of wolves like those newspaper guys. How did they take it? Did you find out who Aunt Fanny really is?"

"There was just one guy," Chrissy said, walking down the hall toward her cousin, who was still leaning around the door. "He's the editor, I gather. Jay Kramer—do you know him?"

"Jay Kramer?" Caroline asked. "Jay? Oh, I know him, all right. He's in my biology class. Isn't he funny?"

"I guess so," Chrissy said, noting Caroline's broad smile.

"He has a wicked sense of humor," Caroline went on. "You should see the way he baits our teacher."

"I can imagine," Chrissy said dryly.

"Did he give you a bad time?"

"He thought I was pretty funny," Chrissy said, "but he came around to appreciate my point of view, I think. Either that, or the whole thing is one big joke on me."

An alarming thought flashed through her mind as she said this. *Is Jay really only leading me on about writing the column, just so he can make fun of it? It's hard enough to tell with regular city kids when they are teasing and three times as hard with someone like Jay.*

"Did you find out who Aunt Fanny is?" Caroline asked again, with a grin.

Chrissy nodded. "He wrote it himself," she said. "As a joke, just like you said."

"He would," Caroline agreed. "Everything's a joke to him. But he is kind of cute, don't you think? I like his curly hair."

Chrissy considered her cousin's comments. "I hadn't even thought about it. I guess he is okay. Not my type, though. I don't like guys who make me uncomfortable, and I get the feeling this guy is laughing at me behind my back."

She went to open the bedroom door, but Caroline blocked her way.

"What's the matter?" Chrissy asked. "Are you hiding something in there that you don't want me to see? Have you smuggled a boy home?"

"Much worse than that," Caroline said mysteriously. "In fact, my father may freak out when he sees this."

She led Chrissy into the room and closed the door behind them. "There, on your desk—do you like it? I bought you a present."

Chrissy walked across to peer inside the glass bowl. A goggle-eyed black-and-gold-speckled goldfish stared back at her.

"Cara!" Chrissy shrieked. As she turned to look at her cousin, Chrissy bumped her hand against the bowl, causing the fish to retreat to the other side. "He's beautiful. It is a he, isn't it? It looks like a guy to me—see his wicked smile! What shall I call him?"

"How about Bug-eye?" Caroline asked.

"Bug-eye? What kind of name is that? I don't want to insult him. I want him to have a wonderful name." She paused to think for a moment. "I know! I'll call him Elvis, because Elvis Presley was the king of rock and roll, and my Elvis is the king of his own fishbowl!"

She rushed across to Caroline and threw her arms around her. "Thank you! Thank you! Thank you!" she sang. "You are so nice!"

"Chrissy, it's only a goldfish," Caroline gasped as Chrissy squeezed her tightly.

"But he's my own pet, and he can sit on my desk while I'm doing my homework, and I can tell all my problems to him."

"Then why don't you call him Aunt Fanny?" Caroline asked, straightening her hair as Chrissy let go of her to gloat over the fish again.

"He doesn't look like an Aunt Fanny. Definitely an Elvis," Chrissy said, "and I think it was great of you to go out and get him for me. I spent half the day trying to think if I'd ever seen a pet shop in the city."

"I wanted to cheer you up," Caroline said. "You wanted a pet so much and the others were all teasing you about it." She came and peered over Chrissy's shoulder. "I must admit," she said, "he is kind of cute. Look at those pretty fins, all shimmering, and he has such interesting bubble eyes."

"Do you think your folks will really mind?" Chrissy asked, looking up nervously.

"What can they object to?" Caroline replied. "He can live in here, where they'll never have to see him, and he doesn't bark and he hasn't got hair to be allergic to, and nobody has to take him on walks. All in all, he's the perfect pet."

"You hear that, Elvis? You're the perfect pet," Chrissy said. She grinned at Caroline, then gazed back into the bowl. "You're going to be a good little fishy for Auntie Cara, aren't you, my sweetie pie?" She put her face near the glass and began to make loud kissing noises as the fish swam toward her. Caroline shook her head in disbelief as she turned to walk from the room.

"Any day now I'll be writing to Dear Aunt Fanny about my weird cousin who's fallen in love with a goldfish!" she said.

"I have to have someone to love me right here," Chrissy called after her. "My boyfriend is a thousand miles away."

"You're right." Caroline poked her head back in through the doorway. "Everybody needs somebody to love them. Maybe I'd better buy myself a goldfish, too."

"You could buy yourself a girl and we could breed them!" Chrissy yelled delightedly.

"Not a great idea, Chrissy. My folks might

overlook one goldfish, but I don't think they'd go along with fish eggs in the kitchen sink," Caroline said as she turned toward the door. "You just keep Elvis. I'll stick to my teddy bear."

As soon as Caroline had shut the door behind her, Chrissy gave Elvis's bowl one more kiss, then went to work on creating her first column. Since there were no real letters to Aunt Fanny yet, Chrissy had to invent her own, and she didn't know where to begin.

As she sat there chewing on a pencil, conscious of Elvis's bug-eyed stare, she mulled over all the little worries she'd had this year and how they had managed to resolve themselves. She wriggled in embarrassment upon remembering how she had tried to act like a sophisticated snob to impress Hunter and his group. She remembered how hard it had been to fit in, how hard it had been to cope with loneliness, even how hard it had been to stay on her diet! They had all seemed like enormous problems at the time, yet they had all solved themselves.

Maybe that's the answer, Chrissy decided. *Maybe most problems do just solve themselves in time. It's all a matter of common sense. I'll just try to think of what sort of answer Grandma Madden would give if I came to her with a problem. She'd say things like, Stop trying to be somebody you're not, girl; Be true to yourself; Trust your own judgment . . .*

Chrissy started to write. Her advice was in no way slick or sophisticated or humorous, but it sounded as if Grandma Madden might have given it—the sort of advice she would have received back home, not in this sophisticated city.

The next morning she took the column, very hesitantly, down to the newspaper office. She fervently hoped that someone other than Jay would be there—that she could just leave the envelope on Jay's desk. But, once again, he was the only person working.

"Aunt Fanny in person—how exciting!" he said jokingly as she closed the door behind her. "I can't wait for the first column. Did you invent some really juicy problems?"

Chrissy ignored his remark and came back with one of her own. "Do you live down here?" she asked. "Don't you ever leave?"

"Well, you see," he replied smoothly, "I'm actually a poor orphan with nowhere else to go, and I get my education and food on the condition that I edit the newspaper for the rest of my life. I haven't been upstairs to see the sunshine for three years now. That's why I can't seem to get along with girls. Do you think Aunt Fanny could help me?"

"I doubt it," Chrissy said. "Some people are past helping."

Jay nodded. "That's me—past helping," he agreed. "Is that the column you've brought?" He held out his hand. "The envelope, please . . ." He took it from her. "And the winner is . . ." he went on.

Chrissy watched nervously as his eyes ran down the page. "Boy, this is serious stuff! I don't think the readers are going to buy this. 'Don't try to be someone you're not, because that way you can't like yourself, and you have to live with yourself every moment of every day.'" He looked up, his amused eyes meeting hers. "Well, I said we'll run it for a couple of issues, so we will," he said, "but I get the feeling this belongs back in a *Ladies' Home Journal* from the year 1910. If I can give Aunt Fanny some advice, try and pick some more cool problems. Kids are cool these days, you know. They don't worry about people not liking them. They worry about drugs and booze and sex. Lighten up, will you? These answers sound like a real old Aunt Fanny wrote them from the rest home. Make them witty. Let's get a little humor in there, okay?"

"I can only write the way I am," Chrissy said uneasily. "I wrote about the things that worry me. I guess I'm not like the rest of the kids here. You don't have to run the column if you don't want to."

"I said I'd run it," Jay replied, "but don't be surprised if you see half the school cracking up when they read it! I get the feeling you might be glad your identity is kept secret."

"We'll see," Chrissy replied confidently, although she did not feel at all confident. "You might find you have the hit of the century on your hands!"

Then she turned and walked from the room

with her head held high, not even looking back to see if Jay was laughing at her.

Once she was out in that gloomy, dungeonlike hall, Chrissy's doubts took over. *I know my answers were good answers, for plain, ordinary kids back home*, she thought. *Maybe I am too old-fashioned for city kids. If that's the case, I'll just stop writing the column. I didn't ask to write it; I don't pretend to be a psychology expert or a writer. Anyway, they don't know I'm Aunt Fanny. As long as I can keep my cool, I've got nothing to lose.*

Chapter 6

"Hey! Chrissy, look at this," Tracy called excitedly as Chrissy walked toward the group at lunchtime the following Monday. "Have you seen the new edition of the *Clarion* yet? The editors must have read your mind—they've got a serious Aunt Fanny column this week!"

"A real Aunt Fanny—oh, no!" Randy said in mock horror. "I hope she isn't talking about my problem—I didn't want anyone to know about it."

"Your problems are all censored material," Justine said, giving him a friendly push. "Let's take a look at the paper, Tracy." She positioned herself on the arm of the bench, resting her elbow on Tracy's shoulder, and peered over. "Hey! This isn't half-bad," she said.

Chrissy felt her cheeks burning and pretended to be studying the paper so that they would not notice her flushed face.

"Chrissy was the one who suggested the column," Caroline said. "She went down to the newspaper office and told them what she thought of them."

Tracy looked up with admiration. "Wow!" she said.

"I thought nobody returned from that office alive," Randy added. "I thought they normally found a pile of bones months later."

"Chrissy managed to tame the monsters, from what I hear," Caroline said proudly.

"Is that right, Chrissy?" Justine asked.

"Just one monster. I only spoke to the editor."

"You managed to tame the dreaded Jay monster? He didn't eat you for breakfast?"

"I don't think I'd taste too good to him," Chrissy said, wishing for once that the attention was not focused on her. One tiny slip and she'd reveal her secret identity.

"He couldn't digest her opinions," Justine said, laughing. "Frankly, I'd love to see someone get the better of that guy. He was born sarcastic. He has to make a big joke of everything."

"But don't you think he's cute?" Tracy asked.

"Not my kind of cute!" Chrissy said in horror.

"Oh, I think he has a cuddly teddy-bear look about him," Tracy remarked with a grin. "Don't you think he's cute, Justine?"

"I guess so, in a way," Justine admitted. "Do you think so, Cara?"

Caroline shrugged her shoulders. "I hardly

know the guy," she answered.

"Don't talk about guys being cute," Randy said. "You'll give me an inferiority complex, and then I'll have to write to Aunt Fanny."

"I wonder if real people actually did write these letters," Justine said, still reading the column.

"They sound genuine to me," Tracy said. "I mean, if you were going to invent problems, you'd choose really weird ones, wouldn't you— like 'I think I'm turning into Napoleon' or 'I think I'm a chicken'?"

"Hey! What sort of nut would write stuff like that?" Randy quipped. "Only a brainless idiot would think they were Napoleon, because everyone know that *I'm* Napoleon—and there can't be two of us."

"I wish you'd cool it sometimes," Justine said. "Just take a look at this. This is some real, genuine advice in these answers. I wonder who Aunt Fanny really is. Can't be any of the newspaper staff—they are a bunch of flakes and weirdos. I bet they got in the psychology teacher or something."

"Nah," Randy said, taking the paper from her. "If it was the psychology teacher, he'd have answered that the person only felt lonely because she secretly hates her mother for potty-training her too early!"

Everyone laughed and the conversation passed on to other subjects, much to Chrissy's relief. She felt much better as they walked back to the school for afternoon classes, especially when she considered Justine's reaction to the new Aunt Fanny. Justine was usually so sure about everything, and so ready to put things down. She had done everything and had been everywhere. Even though she was a real city girl, she had approved of the column. She had thought it gave good advice and was worthwhile. *Maybe other kids would, too*, Chrissy thought. *Wouldn't it be wonderful if real letters poured in! Then Jay would have to eat his words!*

"I wonder what kind of kids would write in to a column like Aunt Fanny's," Caroline said as they reached the main steps. "Do you think it would only be the total weirdos, or do you think people like us would ever write?"

"I don't know about you, but my main problem right now is getting enough money for clothes," Justine said, swishing back her lovely blonde hair. "And I don't think Dear Aunt Fanny would just send me a hundred dollars if I asked her!"

The group all laughed.

"I'd write if I had a problem and nobody I could talk to about it," Tracy said, becoming serious again. "It's like a hot line. Even if you don't get an answer, or you don't get the answer you want, at least you've got it out into the open."

"Maybe you're right," Caroline said thoughtfully. "Sometimes there are things too private to discuss with anyone."

With that, they turned and went their separate ways.

In the days that followed, Chrissy was torn between wanting to know if the *Clarion* had received any response to her column, and not wanting to hear that Jay thought of it as a failure. There were times when she actually stood at the top of the basement steps and peered down into the gloom, imagining great piles of letters on Jay's desk, waiting for her to pick them up. She imagined his embarrassed face as he handed them to her and confessed that she had been right all along. But when she actually walked down the first two or three steps, she remembered his sarcastic grin, his cutting words, and she decided to wait awhile before she saw him.

Therefore, she was surprised when a strange boy grabbed her arm as she came out of chemistry class on Wednesday.

"Are you Chrissy?" he asked. "I've been trying to reach you all morning."

"What did you want to see me about?" she asked cautiously.

"Oh, it's not me," the boy said. "I work on the *Clarion* with Jay. He wants to see you in his office. I think he's got something he wants to give you." The boy smirked as if he knew something he wasn't supposed to know.

It took Chrissy a minute to realize that this guy did not know she also worked for the paper and probably thought he was running a romantic errand for Jay.

"Will he be there at lunchtime?" she asked.

"He's always there," the boy replied.

"Thanks," Chrissy answered frostily. "Tell him I'll drop by around one."

"Okay," the boy said, giving her a sickly smile, then disappeared.

Chrissy spent the rest of the morning worrying about why Jay had summoned her. What was it that he had to give her? When she finally pushed open the door, she saw to her annoyance that they were not alone. Jay's messenger was also there, sitting at the typewriter, tapping away.

"You wanted t-to see me?" Chrissy stammered, making very sure she gave no secrets away to the other boy.

"Yeah. I've got something I wanted to give you," Jay said. He picked up a large manila envelope from his desk, then glanced over to the other boy. "Trevor, go get me a slice of pizza at the cafeteria," he said.

Trevor immediately stopped typing and jumped up. "Sure, Jay, right away," he said happily, then bounded off. Jay waited until his footsteps disappeared into the distance before he opened the envelope and poured out its contents. Several letters dropped onto the desk—not the enormous pile Chrissy had dreamed about, but enough to be impressive.

"Holy mazoley!" Chrissy blurted out before she could stop herself. "Are these all for you-know-who?"

"It seems that way," Jay admitted. "Here. Take them and see which ones are worth answering."

Chrissy leaned over to reach the letters, trying

not to grin too obviously. "I can't get over this!" she exclaimed. "Ten letters from the first column. That's terrific!"

"You can't get over it!" Jay exclaimed. "You have just shattered my self-confidence as a news-hound! I never believed anyone would take this seriously. All I can say is that there must be a lot of messed-up kids in this school. A whole school of nut cases running around."

"Just because people have problems doesn't mean they are nut cases," Chrissy said, feeling more secure now that she knew other people took her column seriously. "I don't think you are a nut case."

"That's because I don't have any problems," he declared. "I am perfectly well adjusted."

Chrissy smiled. "You don't know how to take life seriously, I'd say. That can be a problem. Everyone has to grow up someday."

"Not me," Jay replied smoothly. "I'm San Francisco's answer to Peter Pan. I'm never going to grow up, and I'm never going to take life seriously. It's not worth it."

Chrissy didn't answer, but she glanced at Jay thoughtfully as she took the envelope from him. For a moment there had been something in his voice that revealed a feeling of bitterness. Was Jay running away from life because he didn't like it much? *Maybe Aunt Fanny can help you with your problem, Jay Kramer*, she thought as she went out into the dim hallway.

Chapter 7

"Are you home, Chrissy?" Caroline called as she let herself in. Chrissy just had time to stuff the letters under a loose-leaf binder before Caroline flung open the bedroom door.

"Boy, what a workout!" she said, flinging herself down onto her bed. "Every muscle in my body aches. I must have been crazy to think I wanted to do volleyball! I had no idea that all the drills would be like training for the army. They had us flinging ourselves onto a mat today—and it wasn't a very thick mat either. I could still feel the concrete floor underneath it." She lifted her head and propped herself up against the wall. "Have you been home long?"

"Quite a while," Chrissy said.

"I hope you don't mind walking home alone

every afternoon again," Caroline said. "I feel bad about abandoning you. I thought I'd have more free time after I dropped dance classes. . . ."

"You do what you want to after school," Chrissy said. "Just don't suggest that I join you at volleyball. I have delicate bones. They might break if I fling them onto concrete floors."

Caroline laughed wearily. "How about if I tell you that the coach is a tall, gorgeous blond guy with the most incredible muscles and a terrific tan?" she asked. "And he surfs!"

"Is that why you joined?" Chrissy suggested.

"Me? No way," Caroline said firmly. "He's good-looking, but not my type. I thought you might be interested. I prefer brains."

"Do you have any particular brains in mind?" Chrissy asked innocently. "It's been quite a while since you and Alex broke up. . . ."

"Nobody special," Caroline said, flushing slightly. "How about you? Did you get any mail today?"

"No letter from Ben, if that's what you're getting at," Chrissy answered. "I guess I can't hope for more than one letter a month. He's not the greatest writer in the world." As she said this, she remembered the letters stuffed under her binder. Again she imagined Ben's freckled face laughing uncontrollably when he found out that she was Dear Aunt Fanny. . . .

"I am positively starved. I bet I burned a million calories this afternoon. Have you had a snack yet?" Caroline asked, carefully easing herself off the bed.

"Not yet," Chrissy said. "I came straight in here."

"What was so important that you went without food?" Caroline asked in amazement.

"Oh, just my homework. I've got a paper I want to finish," Chrissy answered quickly.

Caroline shook her head in disbelief. "Will wonders never cease? Are you in the process of turning into the Great Brain?"

"Just because I want to get my homework done . . ." Chrissy began uneasily.

"But you're always doing homework lately, every time I see you," Caroline said. "Don't shut yourself away, Chrissy. I want you to enjoy life. Why don't we find you something to do after school?"

"I'm fine, honest I am," Chrissy said. "I have plenty to keep me busy."

"If you say so," Caroline said. "You want me to make you some grilled cheese?"

"I'll get something later," Chrissy said. "You go ahead."

Caroline turned back and eyed her suspiciously. "Too much studying can affect the brain," she said.

"I know that," Chrissy replied sweetly. "Look what's happened to you!"

As soon as Caroline had gone, Chrissy drew out the pile of letters again. She had managed to answer some of them yesterday and wanted to finish the rest so that Jay had plenty of time to include them in the next issue of the *Clarion*. She glanced through the remaining letters. One was from a girl who could not get along with her new stepmother, another who could not get along with her bratty little sister who always borrowed her clothes. Still another was from a girl who had fallen in love with her best friend's boyfriend and didn't know what to do.

Chrissy put down the letters and sighed. Were these people really hoping for magic solutions to their problems? Dear Aunt Fanny couldn't provide magic solutions. One girl was stuck with her new stepmother, and the other girl with her little sister. All they could do was make the best of it. She picked up her pen and began to write:

Dear Fed Up in Frisco,

I'm sorry you and your stepmother aren't getting along, but I bet it's not easy for her either. She's not the one to blame for your parents' splitting up. She has just married a nice man and she's learning to get along with him, to run a new house, and live a new kind of life—only her new husband came with a kid who is making it very clear she's not wanted. That's not giving her a fair chance. You say you've been without a mother for five years. Well, a girl needs a mother when she's growing up. You've missed out on a lot, and now you have a chance for a new mother, but you're rejecting her before she's even started. How would you feel if she walked out and your father was broken-hearted without her? Would things really be better then?

Chrissy paused and rolled her pen up and down her desk. Maybe that wasn't the right answer to give—it looked as though she was taking the stepmother's side, didn't it? *But it's common sense that she's got to learn to get along, for everyone's sake*, Chrissy decided. *Her stepmother can't be a monster. I'm sure she'd want a life with no fights, too!*

She put the letter with her reply to one side and turned to answer the next one.

Dear Confused,

You say that you are madly in love with your best friend's boyfriend and you don't know what to do. As I see it, there is only one thing you can do. If this girl is really your best friend and she's been your friend for a while, doesn't she mean anything to you? Boyfriends often only last a few weeks, but best friends are sometimes forever. If you make a play for him, you could soon find yourself without either of them, and that wouldn't be too smart, would it? I bet you only think you're in love with him because you're jealous that she's found such a cute guy and you haven't. Be happy for her and maybe soon you'll find your own Mr. Right. Then you can go on exciting double dates.

The next morning Chrissy handed the letters to Jay.

"You don't waste any time, I'll say that for you," he admitted as he took them from her. He glanced through them. "I see they're still as heavy as the last ones, but the readers seemed to buy those, so what can I say? We'll just wait and see if this edition gets the same sort of response."

Again Chrissy waited impatiently until the next copy of the *Clarion* came out. Half of her worried that the kids had been interested in Aunt Fanny only because she was something new and she hoped they wouldn't stop writing. Her other half worried that the column would continue and she'd have to keep on writing the answers. She felt her responsibility very strongly and even woke up at night sometimes sweating from a nightmare in which she had given somebody a bad answer. She was still very excited to have this opportunity to help people, but each letter she read reminded her again that she wasn't an expert.

Maybe everything will sort itself out, just the way I've been telling all the people I've written to, she decided, trying to reassure herself. *Maybe the column will be popular for a few more weeks. Then everyone will lose interest and Jay will decide to cancel it. That way I'll have done some good, but it won't be hanging over me forever.*

But the next batch of letters was more than she'd ever imagined. This time Jay really did have a large pile waiting for her on his desk.

"Here," he said, scowling like a little boy. "And don't say 'Holy baloney!' or any of your other weird expressions. These are *all* for you. I guess other people must think Aunt Fanny is a better idea than I do. Still, I suppose even the greatest newsmen are allowed to be wrong once in their lives."

Chrissy suppressed a giggle, and Jay sank back into his chair. "I can't get over this," he said. "How can readers be interested in these boring, trivial problems! Do they really want to read about what to do if their little sisters borrow their clothes, or they can't keep to a diet, or they've broken up with their boyfriend?"

"It seems that way," Chrissy said, quietly taking the letters from his desk. "I'm just as surprised as you are. I thought my answers were probably all wrong—too boring and old-fashioned—but some kids must think they are good, or they wouldn't all be writing to me."

"Perhaps all these letters say Aunt Fanny is full of baloney and should be burned at the stake!" Jay suggested.

Chrissy noticed the familiar sarcastic grin on his face and decided his remark wasn't worth a reply.

She tore open the first letter. "This one is from a girl who can't get a boy to notice her," she said, feeling relief flooding through her.

Jay started to laugh. "Tell her to start walking through the halls naked," he said. "That way everyone will notice her."

"Most amusing," Chrissy answered. "I suppose you're so popular, you've never fallen in love with someone who didn't love you back?"

"Who, me?" Jay answered smoothly. "I never have problems with girls. I just snap my fingers and they line up. When I get tired of one, I take the next in line."

"Did they have to enlarge this doorway to get your head through it?" Chrissy asked sweetly.

"I'm only speaking the truth," Jay said. "Can I help it if I'm irresistible to girls?"

Chrissy looked at him steadily. "Well, I don't know what you do for some girls, but your charms sure aren't working on me," she said.

Chrissy didn't flinch under Jay's mocking gaze. "That's because inside the body of a cute sixteen-year-old, you have the heart of an Aunt Fanny," he said. "I guess romance has just passed you by. That's why you like to get involved in other people's!"

"I'll have you know I have a very handsome boyfriend back home!" Chrissy exploded. "I don't need any romance here, thank you, and if I did, I would want someone a little less conceited than you!"

She turned and stalked out to the sound of Jay's echoing laughter.

I'd just love to teach that guy a lesson, she decided as she strode home, driven down the hill by the strong, blustery wind, *but I'm scared that with anything I try to do to him, he'd get the last laugh!*

Chapter 8

Chrissy let herself into the empty house and hurried through to her bedroom. She couldn't wait to see what challenging problems she had to face this time.

This is one point I've scored against Jay already, she thought as she took out the letters from her backpack. *I've proved him to be wrong about Aunt Fanny. This is a lot of letters. Maybe that's why he's so hostile to me—he knows I've shown him up, and I can tell he hates to be wrong!*

She smiled to herself as she unfolded the letter she had already opened in Jay's office.

Dear Aunt Fanny
I don't know what to do. I have a tremen-

dous crush on a boy in my class. The trouble
is that I'm very shy. How do I let him know
that I like him? I think he likes me a little, but
he's kind of shy, too, and I'm scared he'll run
a mile if he thinks I'm chasing him. I'm so
inexperienced in dealing with boys. Can you
help? Please give me some advice on what to
do next.

                    Signed,
                    Hopeful

*Poor kid, I can understand just what she's going
through,* Chrissy thought as she stared at the
letter. *It must be hard to talk to a boy if you are
shy. I never felt shy when I was at home, but there
have been lots of times since I came here that I
wanted the ground to open up and swallow me
because I felt so foolish.*

She stared at the letter again, feeling strangely
uneasy about it. What was it about the letter that
was worrying her? It was a perfectly normal sort
of problem. It wasn't too serious, and Chrissy was
pretty sure she could help. So why did she feel
there was something strange about Hopeful's
letter? If only she could let Caroline in on her
secret and talk things through with her, everything would be so much easier. Chrissy knew she
wasn't the sort of person who normally kept
things to herself. *I like to talk,* she thought. *I like
to say what I'm feeling and thinking, not like
Caroline, who . . .*

She stopped short and found her hand was

trembling as she held the letter.

Could it possibly be? she asked herself. She got up and walked across to Caroline's desk, where she noticed some of Caroline's homework notes stuffed in her wastebasket. Chrissy straightened out the crumpled sheets and compared the handwriting to that in the letter. She couldn't believe her eyes—it was a perfect match!

Caroline wouldn't write a letter to Aunt Fanny, Chrissy thought, astonished by her discovery. *It's just not like her.*

She studied the letter again, comparing it line by line with the homework notes. Caroline had an interesting way of crossing her *t's*. She made such a long stroke that it often extended through the next letter. "Hopeful" seemed to have the same habit. Also, the capital *C* in "can" had exactly the same curlicue that Caroline added to the *C* in her name. There was no doubt about it— Caroline was "Hopeful."

Chrissy remembered the conversation they'd had about Aunt Fanny with their friends. Caroline had asked if they thought that people like themselves ever sent in letters, or just the weirdos.

But she has me, Chrissy thought helplessly. *She has good friends. She doesn't need an Aunt Fanny; she could have asked any of us for help. We'd all have been happy to put our heads together and come up with an answer. She shouldn't have to write a letter to the local agony aunt.*

Then Chrissy recalled what else Caroline had said that day—that sometimes there were things too private to discuss with anyone.

Perhaps she was afraid we'd laugh or do the wrong thing and blow her chances, Chrissy speculated.

She paused and gazed at Elvis, swimming happily around his bowl. *I wonder who this guy is. Caroline has never even hinted that she liked somebody. How strange she is sometimes. When I had that silly crush on Hunter, the whole world knew about it!*

But Chrissy knew that Caroline did not find it easy to talk about personal things—that was why she had written to Aunt Fanny. She would never have guessed in a million years that Aunt Fanny was her own cousin.

Chrissy smiled to herself at the absurdity of the situation. Would Caroline find it funny if Chrissy told her the truth? Maybe she'd be glad to talk it over. Then they could plan a strategy to get this boy to notice her. It was such a nuisance that Chrissy had promised to keep her identity secret.

I'm going to do my best to help Cara with this, Chrissy resolved. *She needs a new boyfriend— she's been getting over Alex long enough. This new boy will be just the answer!*

Chrissy sat at her desk and took out a clean pad of paper. What could she say that would help Caroline? What advice could she give? She could say all the standard things and tell Cara to act natural around him, to make a special effort to

get to know him as a friend first by asking
questions about his hobbies. But Chrissy got the
feeling that this advice would not be enough. She
had seen Caroline around boys. Her cousin
clammed up, opening her mouth only long
enough for one-word answers that weren't likely
to capture a boy's attention.

*I get the feeling I'm going to have to do
something more drastic in this case*, Chrissy
thought. *I'll set them up in a situation that throws
them together. Then Cara will have to say something, and he will have to notice her. I remember I
did that for Margie Hamilton back home . . . .
Let's see, what did I do then?*

She replayed the Margie Hamilton episode in
her mind. She recalled how she had made Ben
siphon all the gas except a few drops out of
Stefan Riesling's car, then pretended that there
was no room in the truck to give Margie a ride
home. It had been a brilliant scheme. Chrissy
smiled contentedly as she remembered it. Stefan
and Margie, alone in a broken-down car on a
moonlit road, miles from anywhere . . . Chrissy's
smile faded as she remembered the ending to the
scene. Margie had accused Stefan of running out
of gas on purpose. She had yelled at him that she
hadn't thought he was that sort of boy, and she
had walked home, five miles in high heels!

So I wasn't too successful that time, Chrissy
admitted to herself, *but that was last year. I've
become more sophisticated living in the city. I'll
get Cara together with her dream boy and she*

won't even know that it's a setup. Maybe at a party...

She paused again as she realized one thing: She couldn't set up any date until she knew who the mystery boy was. She glanced up to see Elvis watching her intently from his bowl.

"I've got work to do, Elvis," she said to him, bending down to put her face near the bowl. The fish was now used to her and no longer swam away. He fluttered his little fins and continued to stare hopefully at her.

"You see, I've got to find out who this guy is," she told him. "But I've got to be very careful how I do it. Any obvious questions and she'll get suspicious. It will have to be like a detective following up clues."

She stood up and gazed at herself earnestly in the mirror. "Sherlock Madden tackles the most baffling case of her life," she said, giving the mirror an icy stare. "Through sheer logic and brilliant deduction, she manages to solve the mystery of the unnamed boy!" She moved into another pose and another voice. "By Jove! Madden, I don't know how you did it!" "Elementary, my dear Watson, you see, I..."

"Chrissy? Is that you?" Caroline's voice drifted down the hall. Quickly, Chrissy leaped to her desk and snatched up the pile of letters, flinging them under her bedclothes as Caroline pushed the door open.

"Oh, you're alone—I thought I heard voices," she said, looking around the room with a puzzled expression.

"I . . . I was talking to Elvis," Chrissy said hastily. "You know how lonely he gets being stuck here in a bowl all day."

Caroline looked amused. "It sounded as if you were reciting something for him," she said.

"Oh, yes, just some old thing from English class," she said. "He really seems to enjoy poetry. You should see how he wriggles his fins when I recite."

Caroline shook her head and turned toward her bed. She stopped with a puzzled expression when she saw the smoothed-out page of homework notes still lying near her pillow.

"Didn't I throw this in the wastebasket?" she asked.

"Oh, yes, you did," Chrissy said rapidly. "I got it out. I was having trouble with my homework and I wondered if your notes could help me."

"But you're not taking biology," Caroline said.

"No—that's right. I'm not. But I thought those were maybe math notes," Chrissy answered.

They both looked at the page that was clearly covered with writing and not figures.

"Do you need help with math?" Caroline asked. "Show me the problem and I'll go through it with you."

"Oh, don't worry. I managed to solve it on my own, thanks," Chrissy said, giving Caroline her sweetest smile. "You know what they say: 'If at first you don't succeed, try, try again.' Well, I tried again and got it right."

Caroline eyed Chrissy as if she were a being
from another planet disguised as her cousin. She
opened her mouth to say something, then shut it
again.

"So, how was volleyball?" Chrissy inquired
hastily, walking across to her bed and sitting
firmly on the pile of letters under the covers.

"Hard."

"And how was the gorgeous blond surfer
coach?"

"Hmm," Caroline growled. "I don't want to talk
about him?"

"I thought he was so cute."

"Hmm," Caroline said again.

"Have you noticed—there seems to be a total
lack of cute boys around school this semester,"
Chrissy went on, taking out a nail file and
pretending to work on her nails while observing
her cousin closely. "I mean, if I wanted to keep
myself occupied while Ben was far away, I can't
think of a single boy I'd want to go out with. How
about you?"

Caroline shrugged her shoulders. "No, I can't
think of a single boy you'd want to go out with
either," she said smoothly.

Chrissy frowned. Talk about a clam! Caroline
was not going to give a thing away. This case was
not going to be easy, even for Sherlock Madden.
She would have to follow the example of The
Great Detective, and start a systematic search for
clues.

Chapter 9

During the next day at school, Chrissy started her Sherlock Madden investigation, determined to find out who Caroline's secret crush was. She had written herself a logical plan of investigation, just the way she thought Sherlock Holmes would do it. Item number one was to start with the known facts: The boy was in one of Caroline's classes; he probably liked her at least a little; and he was shy. At least that was something to go on—it narrowed down the search from three thousand students at Maxwell to maybe a hundred or so in Caroline's classes.

Next on her list, Chrissy had written Caroline's schedule. Unfortunately, she had none of the same classes as her cousin, but some of their friends did. Maybe, just maybe, Caroline had given herself away by mistake to one of their friends. Maybe she had blushed as a certain boy came by, or made a point of sitting next to him. Chrissy knew that Tracy was in Caroline's first-period math class, so she waited until she and Tracy were walking across the courtyard alone, then mentioned it casually.

"How's your math class these days?" she asked.

Tracy looked puzzled, and Chrissy realized that her question must not have sounded as casual as she'd intended. Tracy shrugged her shoulders. "Fine, I guess."

"You're lucky." Chrissy sighed. "You have the class with the cute boys in it. Mine are all dogs."

Tracy looked at Chrissy in surprise. "In my math class?" she asked. "Cute boys? Who, for example?"

"I don't know," Chrissy said. "I seem to remember that Caroline mentioned something about cute boys in math."

Tracy began to giggle. "Caroline calls that class Nerdsville. In fact, she once asked me if I knew which slimy pond they all crawled out of."

"Oh," Chrissy said. "I guess I must have the wrong class. I remember she came home the other day and started talking about cute boys in one of her classes, and I guess I wasn't listening properly. I'll have to ask her again."

"Why? Are you thinking of changing your schedule? Or are you collecting research material on which classes attract the cutest guys?" Tracy asked with a grin.

"Neither," Chrissy answered, convincingly, she hoped. "I was just looking around my classes today, thinking how gross all the guys were, and I thought to myself that some people had to have more luck than me."

"Not me," Tracy said. "I think guys automatically turn cute the moment they become seniors. They must go through a secret ceremony during summer vacation or something. Maybe they get sent away to a special camp in the mountains where they go in as junior wimps and come out as senior hunks."

Chrissy laughed. "So you go for seniors, do you?"

"I wouldn't be seen dead with a junior," Tracy declared.

"Do most juniors think like that?" Chrissy asked cautiously. "Because I date a junior back home in Iowa. Does Cara feel like that?"

"Cara? I don't know what her type is," Tracy said. "The way she's acting, she's going to pine over Alex's memory until she turns thirty."

They had joined the others for lunch at that stage, leaving Chrissy only with one fact—Tracy knew nothing about Cara's secret crush.

Later that day she tried the same sort of questions on Justine, who was in Cara's French class.

"What is this, some sort of quiz?" Justine asked with a light laugh.

"No. Tracy and I were just comparing notes to see which classes were boring and which at least had enough hunky boys to make them interesting," Chrissy said. "For example, do boys sound better when they talk French?"

Justine burst out laughing. "Are you kidding? When we have to read scenes in French, we all go into hysterics over the accents. The boys are such jerks—they are so afraid of making fools of themselves that they make no attempt at a French accent at all."

"So was it you or Cara who liked a guy in that class?" Chrissy went on while Justine recovered from laughing. "I seem to remember one of you mentioning a guy in that class who's really nice. Whoever it was said she was glad she'd decided to take French and not Spanish."

"I don't remember that," Justine said, "unless it was Pierre."

"Pierre?" Chrissy asked hopefully.

"He was super cute," Justine admitted. "Both Cara and I were hopelessly in love with him."

"*Were?*"

"Yes. He was an exchange student. He went back to France last summer."

"Oh," was all Chrissy could think of to say.

By the end of the day she was no nearer to solving her mystery. She had gathered no information from any of Cara's friends. The only thing she had learned was that Cara was an expert at hiding her true feelings. If her heart beat faster for a boy in one of her classes, then she wasn't letting it show.

I'll just have to spy on Cara myself, Chrissy

decided. *I still don't know about the boys in her biology and P.E. classes.*

So the next afternoon, as Caroline left English for biology, Chrissy watched her from the shadows. She waited until two large boys walked past behind Caroline, then slipped into place behind them. She followed Caroline down the English hall, down the stairs, along the science hall toward the labs. The two boys turned off to the physics room and Chrissy was suddenly alone in the hall behind Caroline. She crept behind her cousin, her sneakers making no sound on the tile floor. *Maybe if I'm quiet enough, I can observe Cara actually going into biology and see how she acts, and how the boys react when she walks in,* Chrissy thought.

Caroline reached the door of the biology lab with Chrissy only two paces behind her. Then, without warning, Caroline turned around and glanced back down the hall. Chrissy swung toward the bulletin board and pretended to study one of the notices.

"Hi, Chrissy. What are you doing here?" Caroline asked in a surprised voice. "Don't you have English class upstairs right now?"

"Oh, there was a notice here I had to come and read," Chrissy said, not taking her eyes off the board. Caroline came to stand behind her.

"You are thinking of trying out for the boys' wrestling team?" she asked in a voice that was half-amazed and half-amused.

"The what?" Chrissy asked in surprise, realizing for the first time what the notice was announcing. "Oh, no, I just thought I might go along and watch the tryouts. All those masculine bodies in little body stockings . . ." She gave Caroline a mischievous smile.

Caroline just stood in the hall staring at her. "Hadn't you better hurry? You'll be late for English," she said. "I know Mrs. Grant hates people to walk in late."

"Oh, yes, Mrs. Grant. I'd better hurry," Chrissy said and began to walk back down the hall, conscious of Caroline's eyes following her. She barely even noticed Jay Kramer, hotshot newsman, running past her for the biology room.

Cara's getting suspicious, she thought gloomily. *I'd better be more careful on my next spying mission. I just know she will appreciate this when she gets together with her secret crush.*

Chrissy really wanted to spy on Caroline during P.E., because P.E. was one of the only classes in which Caroline would meet seniors, and if she felt the way Tracy did, only seniors would be of interest to her. If P.E. had been in one of the fields across the street, it would have been very simple to slip out and wander along in a stream of pedestrians, watching through the wire fence as she strolled. But during the wet season, P.E. was held either in the gym or on the blacktop beyond it. Chrissy happened to know that Caroline's class was out on the blacktop on Tuesdays and Thursdays, because her own P.E. class had the same schedule of activities. They would be playing hockey and the class would be mixed—boys and girls!

As Chrissy sat through Mrs. Grant's reading of "some fine examples of contemporary American poetry," she plotted her strategy for Monday. The blacktop area was enclosed by brick walls in three sides, so the only place a person could watch unobserved would be a tiny window high up in the girls' locker room. Since her chemistry class was just around the corner from the locker room, Chrissy would have a viable excuse to use the bathroom there. Of course, she would have to cut class, but for some reason Mr. Mathews seemed to like her, so she didn't think she'd get in too much trouble.

The plan worked smoothly. Her chemistry teacher hardly paid attention on Monday morning when she asked to leave the room. She ran to the locker room, climbed up on the toilet tank nearest the window, and moved cautiously across the wooden shower partitions, grateful that her childhood had included so much tree climbing. Finally she perched between the second and third showers and leaned across to gaze out the window. There was Cara's P.E. class! She could see Cara's neat ash-blonde hair, tied back in a cute ponytail. She looked so dainty and elegant as she ran down the blacktop with her hockey stick. Chrissy followed her every movement. After ten minutes the only contact she had with any boys was when she collided with a big football player who was blocking her way. It was clear that the boys were determined to hog the ball and were paying little attention to the girls. Meanwhile, the girls ran hopefully up and down the blacktop, trying for a whack at the ball, even trying to steal it from their male teammates. Finally Cara was called out and a substitute girl was sent in her place. She remained on the sideline, huddled by the brick wall with a few other girls until the bell rang.

This might be the critical moment, Chrissy decided, peering more closely. *As they leave, maybe she will exchange a smile or a few words with her mystery crush.*

She traced Caroline's progress across the yard. She watched her pick up her sweater and join the other girls heading toward the building. It was only when Chrissy heard the sound of their voices that she realized she was trapped in the locker room. *Holy mazoley!* How am I going to get myself out of this mess? She thought in a panic as she slithered down into the shower stall. She hastily locked her door just as the noisy, laughing group came in.

"Did you see what he did, the creep?" a voice was asking. "He just ran with his hockey stick stuck out, tripping up people. Some nice guy, eh?"

"Those guys are all creeps. Did you notice that they didn't pass the ball once? I was wide open and I kept yelling to Kevin and he passed to Scott instead, who of course lost the ball instantly."

"So what's new?" Caroline's voice joined in. "When do they ever pass to girls in P.E.? It would be so much nicer if we could have girls' P.E. separately."

"I agree—it would be nicer. But we've got to prove that we're just as good as those dumb macho boys. It's not equal opportunity if we can't do all the sports boys can."

"Oh, I want to do all the sports," Caroline said firmly, "just not with boys."

The door beside Chrissy slammed, making her jump. She heard water gushing out of the shower in the next stall and some trickled through the space under the doors, lapping around her feet. She stepped back in alarm, moving her feet to the higher ground at each side of the drain. Then someone tried her door.

"Hey! This door's stuck," a voice complained.

"Use another shower."

"But this is the only other one with hot water. Remember, we could only get cold out of those down there, and I'm absolutely desperate for a shower."

The girl shook the door to Chrissy's stall so hard that Chrissy wouldn't have been surprised if she had pulled it right off the hinges.

"Why don't we get the janitor?" someone suggested. Chrissy's heart did a rapid somersault.

"I don't want the janitor in here while I'm changing," someone else argued.

"Let me see if I can slip in under the door," Chrissy heard her cousin offer. "Maybe it will open from the inside."

Chrissy quickly looked around the stall. Could she vault up to grab onto the top of the partition? Or haul herself up the shower head? Or even slip through the three-inch space between showers? Before she could decide, Caroline's face appeared under the door.

"It's no good, I'd never get through here," she said, "It's much too . . .

She looked up directly into Chrissy's embarrassed face.

"Hi," Chrissy said weakly.

Caroline blinked and looked at Chrissy again. "What on earth are you doing in there?" she asked.

"Is there someone in there? Who is it? It's not a boy again, is it?" Voices babbled outside the door. Caroline's head slid back.

"No, it's not a boy—it's Chrissy," she replied uncertainly, as if she still couldn't believe what she had seen. "She's standing in the shower with all her clothes on."

Meekly, Chrissy unlocked the door and tried to ignore all the pairs of eyes watching her expectantly.

"I . . . er . . . got trapped in here," Chrissy said. "I . . . uh . . . came in to look for my barrette, which I thought I dropped after P.E., and I was just looking down the drain, in case it fell down there, when I heard your voices and one of them sounded like the teacher . . . so uh . . . I thought I'd better hide in case I got into trouble, because I didn't want her to yell at me for hanging around where I shouldn't be. I know how mean she is."

"Chrissy, we have a man teacher," Caroline said calmly. "He's not going to come into the girls' locker room."

"Oh ... silly me," Chrissy babbled. "Imagine getting all scared for nothing. Well, I'd better be getting back to chemistry or I'll get in trouble there."

She turned to hurry out.

"What about your barrette?" one of the girls called after her.

"My what?"

"Your barrette—you said you were looking for it. Do you want us to keep our eyes open? What color is it?"

"Oh, don't bother. It was nothing. Just an old one, and I bet it went down the drain. That's what they always do, isn't it?" Chrissy babbled on. "'Bye, see ya later, Cara."

"Is she always weird like that?" Chrissy heard someone ask as she ran out.

Chapter 10

Chrissy arrived home breathless, having run most of the way. She had not wanted to risk running into Cara and the rest of the gang on their way out of school, as she was afraid Caroline would have questioned her about the shower episode in front of the others. It had been very clear from Caroline's expression earlier that she did not, for one minute, believe Chrissy's lame explanation about looking for a barrette.

"I really blew that, Elvis," she told her goldfish as she sprinkled food into his bowl. "Now she's really suspicious. I don't see how I'll be able to find out who the boy is now. It's hopeless. She hasn't said a thing to any of her friends, and I can't go spying on her anymore. Maybe I'd just better give up and answer some more of my Aunt

Fanny letters."

Chrissy was busily writing her advice to "Wanna Be Cool," when Caroline came in.

"More homework?" she asked. Chrissy slid the letter into her chemistry book.

She nodded. "I like to get it out of the way early so I can watch TV."

"Chrissy, I want to talk to you," Caroline said, "because you've been acting very strangely."

Chrissy looked up. "Just because I was in the shower today. I have a perfectly logical explanation. . . ."

"Not just in the shower, Chrissy," Caroline said. "You seem to have changed. You've become secretive about your own life, yet you've been nosing into mine. You were going through my wastebasket last week. Then you followed me down the hall. I want to know what's going on, Chrissy."

"Nothing's going on. It was all coincidence. Just because I happen to meet you a few times around school . . ." Chrissy began hotly.

"So no one asked you to spy on me?" Caroline asked.

"Of course not!"

"I just wondered," Caroline said. She sat down and sighed. "Maybe I'm getting paranoid. I was beginning to tell myself all sorts of dumb things."

"Like I was working for the CIA?" Chrissy asked with a grin. The ridiculousness of the whole situation was beginning to occur to her.

"Like maybe you had been invited to join a

secret society at school. I've heard rumors about them, you know. I thought maybe this was part of your initiation."

"To assassinate my cousin?" Chrissy asked.

Caroline shook her head and smiled. "So I was being dumb," she said. "Overreacting as usual. Why should I worry if my cousin follows me around all day? But you must admit that you have been acting weirdly, Chrissy. It's just that your personality seems to have changed. All this homework suddenly, and talking to a goldfish. You're not in any sort of trouble, are you?"

"Me? No, I'm just fine. Everything's just fine."

"Okay," Caroline said reluctantly, "but you know you can tell me anything, don't you?"

"The same goes for you," Chrissy said. "You can always tell me anything."

"Thanks," Caroline said, getting out her binder from her schoolbag. "It's good we've got each other, isn't it? I have a ton of homework tonight. If I don't get started right away, I'll be working until midnight. . . ."

She opened her binder and began to work. Chrissy attacked her own chemistry at her desk. For a while there was complete silence in the room. Then Caroline thumped her book down and got up. "It's no use. I'm starving," she said. "I need a snack before I die of starvation."

"I'll get you one," Chrissy said kindly. She had been feeling badly about spying on Caroline, even if it was all for her own good. "What would you like? Shall I open a can of soup?"

"That would be great," Caroline said. "How about clam chowder?"

Chrissy went out to prepare the soup, and returned with two big earthenware bowls on a tray and a slice of bread beside each. "Here you are," she said. "Where do you want me to put it?"

"I'll make room," Caroline said, moving her binder across the desk. Chrissy put the bowl carefully onto the desktop and then carried the tray to her own desk.

"You are terrific sometimes," Caroline said. "This was just what I wanted."

Chrissy lowered the tray to the surface of her desk with trembling fingers. She could hear the spoon rattling against the earthenware.

"I'm glad you take good care of me," Caroline went on, dipping her spoon into the bowl.

"I'm glad, too," Chrissy said with a smile. *Because if I hadn't brought that bowl of soup to you at your desk*, she thought, *I'd never have seen what you had drawn on your binder paper*! It was tiny, almost too tiny to read, in one corner. But it was unmistakably a heart, and inside it, Chrissy had found an unexpected clue. Inside the heart, Caroline had written "C loves J."

She glanced up at Caroline. Her cousin was eating contentedly. She probably had no idea that the doodle was on her page, or that Chrissy would have noticed it.

Now all I have to do is find out who J is, Chrissy thought excitedly.

"Volleyball gets worse and worse," Caroline

said between mouthfuls. "Do you know what Jason wants us to do?"

"Jason?" Chrissy squeaked.

"The coach. The cute surfer guy I told you about. He wants us to jog two miles before practice. Does that sound like torture or what?"

Was Jason the one? Chrissy wondered. Had Caroline joined volleyball only because she had a crush on the coach?

"But doesn't having such a cute guy as a coach make it all worthwhile?" she asked, trying to keep her voice light and teasing. "Wouldn't the girls do anything for him?"

"Some of the girls might," Caroline said. "Some of the girls really go for that terrific tan and bleached-hair stuff."

"But you don't?"

"All I see is a monster with a terrific tan and bleached hair," Caroline said. "I like my guys to show a little heart, not to keep yelling 'faster, faster' when I'm staggering around the running track!"

Chrissy laughed and mentally crossed Jason off the list. If Caroline really liked him, then she was one terrific actress!

So all I have to do is go systematically through her classes and find out how many boys have names that begin with J, she decided. *It shouldn't be too hard to get class lists, or to ask Tracy.*

But by noon the next day, Chrissy had to admit that her task was not going to be easy. The first class she had investigated had two Johns in it, a Jimmy, a Joe, a Joshua, and a Jose. Chrissy felt daunted. She could hardly spy on six boys from one class and then multiply that number by six! It would take all semester, and by that time Caroline would either have become engaged to the boy or gotten over him!

She was walking down the hall with Caroline the next afternoon when a breakthrough finally occurred. As they passed the basement steps, Caroline paused and peered down into the gloom.

"You know, I've never been down there in all my years at Maxwell," she said.

"You haven't missed much," Chrissy answered casually. "It's only water pipes overhead and a long dark hallway leading nowhere."

"Maybe I'll get up the nerve to go down there before I graduate," Caroline said. "I really should, in the interests of research, don't you think?"

"Not unless you're thinking of signing up for wood shop or writing something for the newspaper, or cleaning out the broom closets," Chrissy said.

Caroline looked at Chrissy with a curious expression. "You sound as if you know the place pretty well," she said. "Have you been down to visit the newspaper more than once? Justine thought she saw you going down last week."

"Oh, last week, huh? Maybe I did. . . ."

"'Have you found yourself a new interest or do you just enjoy fighting with the editor?" Caroline asked. "Do you still think he's a monster?"

"He doesn't scare me one bit," Chrissy said. "I can defend myself pretty well in any fight with him, and he knows it!"

"You sound as if you enjoy going down there to visit," Caroline said, with a hint of suggestion in her voice.

"Hey! You make it sound as if I'm hanging around there all the time," Chrissy protested, feeling her cheeks turning pink. "I've only been down to . . . to tell him he was doing a good job by following my advice. It was a chance to score a point. Jay Kramer needs someone to keep him in line. He . . ."

Chrissy broke off in mid-sentence. She realized that what she had just said was somehow significant. Something had rung a bell in her head; but what? She gazed down the dark stairway, then suddenly snapped her head up to look at her cousin. Could it be . . . Jay Kramer? The bell had started ringing as soon as she had mentioned his name. And Caroline was still lingering, peering down the stairs. What had she written on her paper? *C loves J?* Why else was she suddenly so interested in what went on downstairs?

All the pieces seemed to fit. Chrissy recalled Caroline's interest when she'd first spoken of visiting the paper. She had mentioned—casually, of course—that he was in one of her classes and admitted that he made her laugh. When all the other girls had been discussing whether he was cute, Caroline had been strangely silent. Had she deliberately kept herself out of the discussion because she didn't want to give herself away? But Caroline had admitted privately that she liked Jay's curly hair.

Of course Caroline might fall for someone like him, Chrissy thought. *He is very quick-witted, with that slick sort of humor that city girls go for. Caroline even said she prefers a boy with brains— but shy?*

She almost laughed out loud. Shy was certainly not how she would describe Jay Kramer! He had the biggest ego Chrissy had ever come across. And yet . . . could that slick exterior and all that self-confidence really hide a shy person that only Caroline had recognized? Chrissy recalled the one or two hints of insecurity Jay had revealed. Maybe he was like Caroline—very good at hiding his true feelings. Maybe they did belong together!

Don't worry, Cara, help is on the way, Chrissy said to herself. *Aunt Fanny will arrange everything. Soon you and Jay will be living happily ever after!*

Chapter 11

Now that she had solved the Great Boy Mystery, Chrissy felt a great sense of accomplishment, and she was looking forward to the next step of her plan with growing excitement. It should be the simplest thing in the world to get Caroline and Jay together, only she would have to be subtle about it, because they were both very smart people. Chrissy also knew that neither of them would take kindly to interference, so their meeting would have to seem natural.

Chrissy racked her brains for a place where she could arrange a romantic rendezvous for Caroline and Jay. Cara had told her they were in the same biology class, but with all those dissected animals around, that wouldn't be very romantic. Chrissy considered the idea of having a party, but then decided against it. The last party she'd thrown had been for Halloween, and everyone had had a terrific time—except Caroline. That was the night Alex had met his new girlfriend, and the last thing Chrissy wanted to do was to bring back those memories for Caroline.

She thought of other occasions when a boy could usually meet a girl. There was a ski weekend coming up at school—but what if Jay didn't ski? What if he didn't like the cold? Besides, Chrissy was not a skier herself. She could hardly arrange a romantic meeting on the slopes when she was looking to grab hold of the nearest tree or falling down in the snow.

There must be someplace where I can stay in charge of things, she mused. *Somewhere romantic, yet not too obvious.*

Then the perfect occasion arose. She ran into a girl she knew from the dance chorus of the musical last term. Nancy was now active in the glee club and mentioned that the group was planning a Fifties-style sock hop to raise money for the spring concert.

"I hope you're going to come with all your friends," Nancy said.

"Oh, I don't know," Chrissy answered hesitantly. "I'm not sure I've got anyone to come with."

"Oh, come on," Nancy insisted. "It's not a couples thing. Plenty of people will be coming without partners. Just bring a group of friends."

"I'm not sure that my friends would . . ." she

began, when it suddenly hit her. What more
perfect place to get Cara and Jay together than a
dance! Fifties music, slow rock, soft lights. It was
ideal.

"Great idea, Nancy! I'll be there," she said, then
ran off as Nancy stared after her.

*Now all I have to do is convince Caroline and
Jay that they both want to come to the dance*, she
thought *and that might not be too easy!*

She tried Caroline first, as she was not exactly
looking forward to tricking Jay into coming to a
dance, and besides, the whole plan would be
useless if Caroline wouldn't go.

"Oh, I don't think so, thanks, Chrissy," Caroline
said when Chrissy excitedly told her about the
dance. "I mean, I don't have anyone to go with. I
hate feeling like a wallflower."

"But I don't have anyone to go with either,"
Chrissy pleaded. "We could be wallflowers together."

Caroline shook her head. "I know you," she
said gloomily. "You'd be at the dance less than
two minutes and you'd pick up a gorgeous guy.
Then I'd be left alone to be a wallflower without
you."

"Cara, I wouldn't do that," Chrissy said. "I
promise, if any guy asks me to dance, I'll make
him go get his friend for you before I say yes."

Caroline laughed. "That's nice of you, but I
don't think I want to be a threat held over
someone's head. I don't know, Chrissy. Since
Alex . . ."

"Since Alex you haven't dated anyone, I know," Chrissy finished for her. "You need to get your self-confidence back. You need to see that there are plenty of other cute guys in this school, just waiting to dance with you. Come on, Cara, say you'll come to the dance with me. I really want to go—Fifties music is my favorite! You know good old Elvis and all that ba-ba-ba and sha-boom, sha-boom stuff. I'm crazy about that."

"You go then, Chrissy," Caroline said. "I'm not stopping you."

"But I don't want to go alone," Chrissy said. "I don't enjoy being a single wallflower either."

Caroline smiled. "I've never known you to be shy—especially when it comes to cute boys," she said. "You'd do just fine without me there."

"No, I wouldn't. I'd hide in a corner and not speak to a soul."

"That would be the day! Chrissy Madden, you've never kept your mouth closed for longer than thirty seconds. I'm the shy one, remember!"

"I know I'm not shy by nature," Chrissy retorted, "but since coming here, I've found so many things that are different. You know I hate to look like a fool, Cara. Please come with me. We can stay only a little while if you like, and then we'll leave. Please, Cara?" she implored.

Chrissy turned her head to one side and made what Caroline called her sad little puppy dog face—the one that always worked on her father when she had run out of her allowance before the end of the month. It usually worked on her cousin, too, and this time was no different.

Caroline shrugged her shoulders and smiled nervously. "I suppose you'll give me no peace until I agree to come with you," she said. "You are a big pest. Do you know that?"

"Oh, yes, I know," Chrissy said happily. "My brothers used to tell me that every day back home. But you won't regret this, Cara. You'll be so glad you decided to come."

"Why?" Caroline asked suspiciously.

"Because ... uh ..." Chrissy said haltingly, caught off guard, "because you might meet the man of your dreams, just waiting for you to show up."

Caroline laughed again. "With my luck, Chrissy, some five-foot nerd with a squeaky voice will follow me around all evening, and I'll end up dancing with him even though he only comes up to my shoulder."

"Then I will nobly take him off your hands and leave you to dance with his six-foot friend," Chrissy said.

"I'll believe that when I see it," Caroline said. "And I hope you have some great ideas about what we can wear to a Fifties dance. I've never been to one."

"Neither have I," Chrissy said. "That's why I want to go so much. That's why it will be so much fun."

But Caroline did not look totally convinced.

The next day Chrissy tackled the task of inviting Jay to the dance. This was much harder than persuading Caroline, because she never felt at ease with Jay. She felt all the time as if they were having a fencing duel and she had to be constantly on guard for a sneaky stab. Jay would definitely be suspicious—of that she was sure. After all, she had made it clear that she didn't like him too much. Wouldn't he think it strange that she suddenly wanted him to go to a dance? She'd have to be careful.

That morning, she found Nancy. "I think I can sell some of those tickets for you," she offered. Nancy gladly handed the tickets over. Then, holding the tickets in front of her like a shield, Chrissy went down to the basement to seek out Jay. Fortunately, he was alone this time, as Chrissy had dreaded having to invite Trevor as well. Jay would be suspicious if she didn't.

Jay looked up in surprise as she came in. "You're early with copy this time, aren't you?" he asked. "We don't do layout until the beginning of next week."

"I'm here on official business," Chrissy said, waving the tickets. "I was the only person in the entire club brave enough to come down here. Everyone else turned pale at the thought."

Jay laughed. "Is our reputation that bad?"

"Rumor has it that nobody returns from this office. I'm the only person in recorded history to have survived to tell the tale."

"Oh, really—I'm supposed to be as fierce as all that, am I?" he asked.

"Oh, no—that has nothing to do with it," Chrissy quipped. "It's just that this office is such a mess, strangers can never find their way out again. But I happen to be a messy person, too, so this is a piece of cake compared to my room at home."

Jay leaned back in his chair and balanced against the filing cabinet, then looked up at her. "Okay, what is it you're trying to sell me?" he asked. "Raffle tickets for the home for unmarried mothers or lost dogs?"

"Neither. Tickets for the glee club dance."

"The glee club dance?"

"Yes. You see, the glee club is raising money for their spring concert and they are having a Fifties-style sock hop. Each member has to see ten tickets. I've already sold nine, and I thought of you. You look like the kind of guy who'd like to do Fifties-style dancing."

"Me? I can't dance," Jay said hurriedly.

"There's nothing to it. You just stand there and sway. I'll teach you," Chrissy offered.

Jay gave a short laugh. "I know you," he said. "You'd wait until I was off balance, then push me over or something."

"Jay, I wouldn't do a thing like that."

"Besides," he said, "I can't think of a girl I could bring . . . who would enjoy that type of dancing, that is. Most of my girl friends are more sophisticated. They are used to glamorous nightclubs, not high school sock hops."

"Of course," Chrissy said. It had been on the tip

of her tongue to challenge Jay the stud's ability to find a girl to bring. Luckily, she had stopped herself in time. The last thing in the world she wanted to do right was to discourage Jay from coming, or even worse, goad him into finding another girl!

"Don't worry," she said smoothly. "There will be plenty of cute girls just dying for the chance to dance with you." Chrissy noticed that Jay looked interested now. "I'll be there," she went on "and I don't have anyone to dance with. And several of my friends will be there, too."

Jay tipped his chair upright so that it clomped noisily onto the floor. "Why the hard sell to me?" he asked, looking her in the eye. 'Don't tell me I'm the only guy in the school who hasn't bought a ticket from you."

Chrissy searched her brain rapidly for the right answer. "I . . . er . . . thought of you because you are such a fun person. We need lots of fun people to keep the evening going. The . . . er . . . glee club suggested your name, in fact."

Jay continued to look at her steadily—so steadily that she could feel the blush spreading over her cheeks. *He thinks there's a catch to this; I can tell*, she thought. *He won't come and it will all be for nothing*!

"I'd better be getting along," she said, turning away hastily. "I've still got tickets to sell."

"Well, aren't you going to leave me mine?" Jay asked as she reached the doorway.

Chrissy spun around delightedly. "You're going

to come? Hey! That's terrific."

His tiger-flecked eyes held hers as he took the ticket from her. "See you Saturday, then," he said.

Chapter 12

"I wasn't sure about coming in the first place, but now that I'm here I'm positively sure I didn't want to come," Caroline hissed into Chrissy's ear. They were standing together at the doorway of the gym, looking at an almost empty dance floor. Only one couple was rocking and a-rolling to the music blaring out over the loudspeakers, while a collection of whispering girls and bored-looking boys bunched against the walls. Only a few had gone to the trouble of putting together a real Fifties outfit, as Chrissy and Caroline had done. With their felt poodle skirts and puffed-sleeve blouses, white socks and ponytails, Chrissy had thought they looked just right before they left the house. Now she felt as if they stood out like two roses in a bed of dandelions.

"What are we doing here? I feel like everyone's staring at us," Caroline said. "And there are no decent guys to dance with here—not one."

Chrissy had to admit that it did not look too hopeful.

"Maybe we're too early," she whispered back, grabbing at Caroline's arm in case Caroline should decide to make a quick getaway. "It will get better later. The kids in the glee club are all fun people."

"Do you see any glee club members here?" Caroline asked, the tone of her hushed voice rising in exasperation. "All they did was sell tickets to all the losers in the school. They are probably off at the pizza parlor enjoying the profits."

"They'll be here," Chrissy said. "Nancy told me she was coming."

"Great—we can take turns dancing with Nancy."

"Hey! Don't be such an old sourpuss," Chrissy said brightly, although she was not feeling too happy herself.

"But I hate coming to dances without a partner," Caroline said. Her gaze went around the walls. "Weird boys come and ask you to dance. And I always do, because I hate to hurt anyone's feelings, but then I find myself trapped with an oddball who wants to show me his computer games or tell me about his tapeworm collection."

Chrissy giggled. "They are not all as bad as that," she said. "And I understand some of the really popular guys will be here later."

"Then they'll come with the really popular girls," Caroline said with a big sigh. "No popular guy would want to admit he couldn't get a date for a dance." She looked at Chrissy pleadingly. "Please, let's go home. I know I'm not going to like this. I don't know what made you think this would be fun."

"What. You want to leave after I paid five bucks for our tickets?" Chrissy asked, keeping a firm hold on Caroline's arm "Come on, Cara. Just give it a try. We could at least eat and drink our money's worth. The food is supposed to be pretty good."

She started to drag Caroline unwillingly into the gym. As they entered, the music switched to a slow number and several couples wandered out onto the floor.

"You see?" Chrissy said excitedly. "People are beginning to dance."

"That's what I'm afraid of," Caroline muttered. "Any minute now the invasion of the nerds will begin!"

"Let's get over to the punch table fast," Chrissy said, realizing that Caroline was right. Several short, wiry boys were eyeing them with interest and trying to act cool, which seemed to be taking a lot of effort.

Before the girls could escape, two boys with padded shoulders and greased-down hair blocked their path.

"Hi, there, beautiful. Wanna dance?" one asked

Caroline, slicking his hand through his hair, then offering the same hand for Caroline to take.

Caroline shrank back against Chrissy.

"Thanks, but she doesn't dance outside her own species," Chrissy said, pulling her cousin away.

"Let's head for that punch table," Chrissy suggested, as they burst into giggles.

"Better yet, let's go to the girls' bathroom and wait in there until normal people arrive," Caroline countered, rushing toward the door at the back of the gym.

The bathroom was crowded with other girls fixing their hair and their makeup. The general subject of conversation seemed to be the lack of unnerdlike boys outside. Chrissy hung back, near the door. Her big fear was that Jay would arrive, take one look inside the gym, and leave.

"I'll see you outside," she whispered to Caroline. "I promised a friend I'd wait by the door."

"Do you mean someone else was dumb enough to accept your invitation?" Caroline remarked, straightening out her ponytail, although it was already perfectly in place.

Chrissy nodded, then slipped back into the gym. More people were beginning to trickle in now, much to her relief. She saw Nancy and several other people from last semester's play. She even saw a couple of basketball players, towering awkwardly over the rest of the kids. Then she saw Jay. He took one step inside the gym, looked around in horror, and turned to walk away. Chrissy sprinted across the floor and grabbed him just as he was disappearing into the night air.

"Hey! Don't go—you just got here," she said breathlessly.

Jay looked down at her with a grin. "That's not my kind of scene in there," he said. "It's too uncool for me."

"I admit it's pretty bad right now," Chrissy said, her eyes pleading with him, "but most of the glee club people aren't here yet. It will get better. Besides, I was waiting for you to dance, with me. You wouldn't want me to be left to those other boys in there, would you?"

Jay's eyes flickered. "Oh, so you've finally decided that I am preferable to some other members of the male sex, have you? You gave the impression before that you wouldn't dance with me if I was the last boy on earth!"

"I did not," Chrissy said defensively.

"What about all those smart remarks you've always made?" he asked, grinning at her as if he was enjoying himself. "You always fight with me."

"I enjoy fighting with you."

Jay laughed. "You're quite a girl, you know that?" he said. "Okay. I'll give it a try, but if it doesn't get better—I'm splitting!"

"You're not going to regret this," she said, leading him triumphantly back into the gym. The disc jockey had just put on a slow number, complete with wailing sax—*perfect for a romantic rendezvous*, Chrissy mused, smiling to herself.

Now all I have to do is find Cara, fast! She
searched the room for her cousin with no luck.
*Knowing Caroline, she's still in the bathroom,
and probably intends to stay there all evening,*
Chrissy thought in a panic.

"Do you think they're playing our song?" Jay
asked with a raised eyebrow.

"If that's our song, then we are doomed for
life," Chrissy said.

"You want to dance anyway?" he asked.

Chrissy took another hasty look around the
gym. She had to keep Jay occupied until she
could find Caroline. "Sure. Why not?" she said,
giving him what she hoped was a convincing
grin.

Jay took Chrissy into his arms and they began
to dance slowly. Chrissy noted with alarm that he
was holding her very tight.

"You know, I can't get over this," he murmured
into her ear. Chrissy could feel his breath against
her cheek.

"Over what?" she asked.

"You—your complete turnaround," he said, giving her waist a little squeeze. "I got the impression we were not getting along too well, and
now . . ."

"Now?" Chrissy asked cautiously.

"I kind of guessed you'd come around in the
end," he declared, giving another little squeeze.
"Most girls do."

"Wait a minute," Chrissy said, hoping that he
didn't mean what she thought he meant. "You

think that I'm chasing you?"

She could feel his laughter. "Well, aren't you? Who invited me to the dance? You don't do that to a boy you aren't interested in."

"But I was just selling tickets for the glee club. I thought you'd be a good person to have here—to make it fun, you know?"

Jay stopped dancing, still holding her very close. "Oh, come on, Chrissy, admit it. That was only a very thin excuse to invite me for yourself, wasn't it?"

"No, it wasn't!"

"You see," he said calmly, "I just happen to know that you don't belong to the glee club. You weren't selling tickets for them!"

"Yes, I was. Ask any members—ask Nancy over there, she'll tell you."

"Chrissy," Jay said calmly, "I'm the editor of the newspaper, remember? We printed a list of all the members of the glee club, so that students would know who they could buy their dance tickets from. I know who the members are."

"Oh," Chrissy mumbled.

"Anyway, why are you denying how you feel about me? You should be glad—everything worked out the way you wanted it to. I'm here, and I'm holding you in my arms, and we're dancing cheek to cheek. Isn't this what you wanted?"

"Well ... uh ... Jay, actually ..." Chrissy stammered. She could feel her cheek, hot and sticky against his. "I thought you really liked somebody else—secretly, I mean."

"Now how would you know what my secret desires are?" he asked teasingly. "I haven't written to Aunt Fanny, you know! Nobody knows the secrets of my heart except me—and right now I'm pretty content to be dancing with you. I thought you looked like a fun girl the moment you walked to my office, you know. I've always enjoyed our little battles of wit."

Chrissy looked around hopelessly. How was she gong to get out of this situation? How could Jay have fallen for her when he was supposed to like Caroline? And how on earth could Cara possibly have a secret crush on Jay? Yuk!

"You know, dancing is pretty boring after a while," Jay murmured in her ear. "What say we leave pretty soon? My car is parked outside. . . ." The way he said it and the way he nuzzled at her ear gave Chrissy a preview of what Jay had in mind, and it was certainly *not* what she had in mind.

To Chrissy's relief, before she could answer, she noticed Caroline come in from the girls' bathroom. As she saw her cousin look around with a worried expression, Chrissy realized that this had rapidly turned into a now-or-never situation. She couldn't let Cara see her dancing with Jay. It didn't matter that she thought Jay was a jerk—if Cara liked him, then she had to get them together.

Chrissy pushed Jay away from her. "Oh, wait a minute, my friend just came in," she said in a rush. "I can't leave her standing all alone. Come on over and meet her. . . ." And before he could protest, she dragged him across the floor, like a small tugboat bringing a liner into dock. Caroline looked up with relief as she spotted Chrissy.

"Thank heavens you're still here," she said. "I thought you'd abandoned me!"

"I wouldn't do that," Chrissy said. "I've brought somebody to meet you. You know Jay, don't you, Cara? And Jay, you know Caroline Kirby."

The magic moment had come. They looked at each other and each smiled politely.

"Oh, hi, Jay," Caroline said.

"Hi . . . er . . . Carla," Jay replied. "Don't I know you from somewhere? One of my classes—you sit right at the back."

"That's right."

Hardly a promising beginning. Maybe they needed a little help.

"Look, I need to pop out to the girls' room," Chrissy announced. "Stick around and keep each other company until I get back." She almost handed them to each other, then vanished into the crowded doorway before either of them could say anything.

Let's see how they get along when I'm not around, she thought. She fought her way into the girls' bathroom and toyed with her hair in front of the mirror. Girls came and went. Chrissy wished that she was the sort of person who used more makeup. She noticed how long other girls took to do their eyes. She glanced down at her watch. Would ten minutes be enough? Better make it a little longer. She didn't want to ruin everything by barging in just when they were getting along.

When she finally returned from the bathroom, Caroline and Jay were standing exactly where she had left them, only she could tell from their faces that things had not been going as smoothly as she had hoped. Caroline was staring up at the revolving mirrored ball that hung from the ceiling and Jay seemed to be occupied watching the dancers.

"Oh, there you are at last," Caroline said when she saw Chrissy. "Where on earth did you go?"

"Were the closest bathrooms at the North Pole, or what?" Jay asked dryly.

Chrissy managed to smile. "Sorry to keep you waiting so long. I . . . er . . . got held up. I met someone I hadn't seen in a while. I thought you two would be getting to know each other."

"So can we please leave now?" Jay asked, touching Chrissy's arm. "I think I've just about had enough of the Fifties."

Caroline grabbed her other arm. "What's all this about going? You're not going to leave me here after you made me stay, are you?"

"Of course not," Chrissy said, feeling she might be torn in half at any moment. Why weren't things happening the way she planned? What could have gone wrong? Was Caroline too shy to admit how she felt about Jay? Had she been wrong in the way she thought Jay felt about

Caroline?

"Why do you want to leave so soon?" Chrissy asked Jay. "You've hardly danced yet. Did you two get a chance to dance while I was away?"

"No," they both said in unison.

"And don't you want to dance now?" Chrissy asked hopefully.

"Er . . . no, thanks," Jay said. "I really want to split. This place is boring me. Are you coming, or what?"

"Just a minute," she said to Caroline. She turned to Jay. "Can I talk to you for a moment?"

He looked at her in surprise.. "Sure."

"Over here," Chrissy said, dragging him into a dark corner, a little way from Caroline.

"Look, Jay," she whispered. "There seems to have been some mixup. I mean, you've got things wrong. I didn't invite you here for myself. I thought that you and Cara . . ."

"You what?" Jay blurted out, loudly enough to make passing couples turn to look at them.

"I thought you liked each other. I know she has a secret crush on you, and I thought you secretly liked her, too."

Jay was eyeing her as if she had turned into some sort of lunatic. "But I don't even know the girl. I see her walk past me to her seat in bio lab, but I don't think I've ever said two words to her."

"Oh," was all Chrissy could think of to say.

"And what made you think she likes me?" he asked angrily. "She gave me the impression that she wanted to get away from me even faster than

I wanted to get away from her."

"I must have made a mistake," Chrissy said miserably.

"So this romantic get-together was your idea?" Jay asked coldly. "I might have known. Just the sort of thing Aunt Fanny would do. So now you're running a dating service as well as solving the world's problems! Very nice. What are you going to do next? Marriage bureau? Adopt-a-pet? United Nations? You seem to like getting yourself mixed up with other people's lives. Is that because your own is so blah? Well, you'd better watch yourself, Miss Meddler, because one day you're going to get yourself into something too big for you to handle."

Then, before Chrissy could say a word, he turned and pushed his way past the crowd of couples rocking and a-rolling, until he was out of sight.

Chapter 13

"Now would you mind telling me what was going on in there?" Caroline demanded as they began walking home in the crisp night air. "What was Jay Kramer doing there? I felt as if I was part of play and nobody had given me the script."

"It's okay. Forget it. It's over," Chrissy said.

"I don't want to forget it," Caroline shot back. "I've just had a very humiliating experience, and I want to know why." She looked angrily at her cousin. "Do you realize that you kept me hanging around with Jay Kramer for twenty minutes while we waited for you? It was so embarrassing I kept wishing the floor would open up and swallow me. Neither of us had a thing to say after we finished discussing the frogs that we are dissecting in biology. And he kept yawning. I know I'm not the most exciting girl in the world, but at least he could have had the courtesy not to yawn What kept you so long in the bathroom?"

Chrissy gave a sigh. "I wanted you and Jay to get a chance to talk."

"For Pete's sake why?" Caroline demanded.

"I thought you were too shy to talk to him, and I figured a dance might set the mood."

Caroline stared at Chrissy, her eyes glinting dangerously under the streetlights. "Set the mood? The mood for what?"

"I thought you liked him," Chrissy confessed miserably. "I guess I misread the signals."

"Signals? What signals? When have I ever given the slightest indication that I was interested in Jay?"

"You asked questions about him the first time I went down to the *Clarion* to see him," Chrissy said, swallowing hard. "You said he was funny. . . ."

"I think George Burns is funny, but I have no desire to go out with a ninety-year-old man!" Caroline almost yelled. "I do think Jay Kramer is funny, but I also think he is a conceited creep. When I'm ready for a new boyfriend, it certainly won't be someone like him."

"I got it wrong," Chrissy said. "I'm sorry. I didn't want to embarrass you. I only wanted to help."

"Who says I need any help?" Caroline asked angrily.

"It was your letter to Aunt Fanny" Chrissy said. "I recognized the writing, you see."

"My letter?" Caroline asked. It came out as a squeak. "You read my letter to Aunt Fanny? What other snooping have you been doing?"

"I wasn't snooping. . . ."

"Oh, no! I thought there was nobody in the house when I wrote that. Did you go through my schoolbag?"

"Of course I didn't," Chrissy protested. "Listen to me, Cara. I am Aunt Fanny."

"You're what?" Caroline came to an abrupt halt. They stood there, facing each other in the yellowish glare of a corner street lamp.

"I'm Aunt Fanny. The letter came to me and I recognized the writing," Chrissy said softly. "I only wanted to help you. I thought I was in a good position to solve your problem. All I had to do was find out who the boy was and arrange a good place for you to meet."

"Oh, wonderful," Caroline said through clenched teeth. "Did you intend to work your way through the entire male population of the school until I was finally face to face with the right boy? It makes me want to die of embarrassment when I think about it!"

"I thought I'd managed to find out who he was," Chrissy said unhappily. "I thought it was Jay. When you stopped to look down the stairs the other day, and you asked what it was like down there, I thought you seemed really interested—interested in the newspaper, and . . . and Jay. I did it for you, Cara. You said in your letter that you were too shy to speak to him. I just wanted to get you started."

"I can't believe you'd do a thing like this!" Caroline said, nearly screeching, striding ahead so rapidly that Chrissy had to run to keep up with her. "My own cousin! Didn't it occur to you that if I wanted your kind of help, I'd have asked you for it? But I didn't, did I? I wanted impartial advice—that's why I wrote to Aunt Fanny. I wanted a person I didn't know to give me some general encouragement—not a step-by-step how-to guide to picking up men! Now I'll never have the nerve to talk to another boy in my life. I'll always be wondering if it's a Chrissy Madden setup."

"Oh, don't be dumb, Cara. So this was one bad experience. I'm really sorry about it—but now that I know about your secret crush, I can give you some ideas to get you together with the right boy!"

"You'll do no such thing!" Caroline said fiercely. "I don't know if you did this sort of thing back home, but here in San Francisco, matchmaking went out of style a few generations ago. So don't you dare try to interfere again, or I'll never speak to you for as long as I live!"

Then she hurried ahead, too fast even for Chrissy to keep up with her. Chrissy watched her go, feeling sick and hurt. She had meant so well. She'd had such high hopes for this evening, but everything had been ruined. She could understand that Caroline had been embarrassed, and that was why she had said so many hurtful things. *But she doesn't have to worry*, Chrissy thought as she watched Caroline disappear around a corner. *I've learned my lesson. I'm going to stick to being impersonal Aunt Fanny in the future—I'm not going to get involved in anyone else's life. Maybe Jay was right. Maybe I am a meddler ... but I come from a place where people like to help other people. I only wanted to do some good with my Aunt Fanny advice. But from now on, I won't tell people what to do. I'll just write some vague comments, and let people figure out the answers on their own.*

For the rest of the weekend Chrissy stayed well out of Caroline's way. This was not too hard to do because Caroline treated her as if she wasn't there. As Chrissy observed her cousin, she realized how very deeply Caroline had been hurt. Chrissy thought of herself as the sort of person who made funny mistakes and did crazy things, and laughed at herself a lot. If the mixed-up date had happened to her, Chrissy would have probably ended up thinking it was hysterically funny and laughing it off with the guy. But she knew Caroline was very different. Cara cared a lot about her image and she hated to look like a fool. As Chrissy watched her walking around the house, tight-lipped and frowning, she felt sorry for her cousin, but she couldn't think of anything to say to make matters better.

All weekend Chrissy tried to be considerate and to show Caroline that she truly was sorry. But by Sunday night her patience was growing thin. She was used to fierce shouting matches with her brothers that were usually resolved within minutes. She didn't like this silent treatment that she was receiving from Caroline.

Finally, her patience snapped. Tracy called on Sunday evening to say that a group of friends were going to see the new movie at the Regency and she asked if Chrissy and Caroline wanted to come along.

"Tracy's on the phone," Chrissy called out to Caroline, who was still finishing her dinner in the kitchen "She wants to know if we're interested in going to the Regency tonight."

Caroline's face appeared around the kitchen door. "Who's going—just Tracy?"

"A group of friends, she said," Chrissy answered. "Just a minute, I'll ask her." She conferred with Tracy and then turned back to Caroline. "About ten of them. Maria and George and Danny and—"

"No, thanks," Caroline interrupted, shaking her head firmly. "I don't think I'll go."

"But why not?" Chrissy covered the phone with her hand. "You said the other day that you really wanted to see *Once Over Easy*, and it got terrific reviews."

Caroline stared at Chrissy with a stony face. "I'd rather not come, thanks. I'm not feeling too great."

Chrissy relayed Caroline's regrets to Tracy and then hung up. "You were feeling fine ten minutes ago," she said. "What's gotten into you?"

Caroline shrugged her shoulders and turned away. "I'm not very keen on going to a movie with you and Tracy and a bunch of strange guys," she said. "Knowing you, you'll probably try to fix me up again. Besides, George was at the dance. He might have seen me and . . . and your obnoxious friend."

"What if he did?" Chrissy demanded loudly. "You are making such a big thing of this, Cara. Why don't you forget it and start enjoying life again?"

"But it is a big thing for me," Caroline retorted, turning her back on Chrissy. "You don't seem to realize how humiliated I felt. I can never face Jay again. I can never face anyone!"

"If you ask me," Chrissy said, following her cousin down the hall, "you are wallowing in self-pity over nothing! You keep saying how embarrassed you were—and for what? Who do you think either knew or cared that you got stuck with a guy by mistake at a dance?"

"What happened must have been very obvious to anybody who saw me," Caroline said in a hurt voice.

"Baloney!" Chrissy replied angrily. "You are getting yourself worked up over nothing. You have nothing to be embarrassed about, and I should know, because I am the champion at having embarrassing things happen to me. What about the time some really cute college guy came to stay with our neighbors and I let him think I was a high school senior when I was really only thirteen?"

Chrissy could tell that she had gotten Caroline's interest, because Caroline paused, halfway through the doorway, and looked back at her.

"And I went to this party with him—you should have seen how dressed up I got and all the makeup I put on, and I had to sneak out without my parents noticing—and guess what? My brother was at the same party and he told the guy the truth about me. The guy got mad and everyone laughed, Caroline. They thought it was the joke of the century. If you want to talk about embarrassed—think of standing in the middle of a circle of people, all pointing at you and laughing themselves silly! And then," she went on without giving Caroline a chance to say anything, "how about the time when I was standing at the top of a pyramid with another cheerleader and she slipped? She grabbed at me as she fell and she ripped my top right off. Have you ever stood in front of a thousand people in your bra?"

"You're making this up," Caroline said skeptically.

"I am not."

"You want me to believe that someone accidentally ripped off your cheerleading uniform in public?"

"You'd better believe it, because it's true," Chrissy declared. "Those uniforms are not made to have a hundred and twenty pounds swinging on them."

"No kidding?" Caroline asked. The ghost of a

smile crossed her face.

"You ask anyone in Danberry if they remember the time. They all do. They still tease me about it."

"So?" Caroline asked uncertainly.

"So I was pretty embarrassed at the time—but I survived. That's what I'm trying to say. We all have embarrassing things happen to us, but we survive. You survived being arrested for standing in front of a bulldozer to save the park, didn't you?"

"Yes, but that was different," Caroline answered thoughtfully. "That didn't make me seem like a fool."

"Well, what about the time I got swept away by that giant wave, the first time I met your friends?" Chrissy asked. "That was pretty embarrassing for me, you know, as well as being scary. Do you think any of your friends held it against me afterward? Did you hear anyone say 'Don't talk to Chrissy Madden, she gets swept away by giant waves'?"

Caroline finally had to laugh. "You are an idiot, do you know that?" she asked, shaking her head fondly at her cousin. "Who else would go to the trouble of trying to set me up with a strange boy?"

"Only someone who cared about you," Chrissy said quietly, "who was sad to see you moping around and dreaming about Alex when you could be having fun with a new boy."

Caroline was silent. She walked ahead of

Chrissy into their bedroom and sat down.

"I was horrible to you this weekend, wasn't I?" she asked, looking down at the floor.

"Not too nice," Chrissy admitted. "But I did understand how you felt. It was pretty awful for me, too. Jay thought I'd invited him because *I* had a secret crush on him."

"Really?" Caroline looked up with a grin. "What did you say to him?"

"I had to tell him that it was all my fault—that I'd made a mistake and that I'd given him the wrong impression."

"I bet he didn't take that too well, knowing the size of his ego."

"Are you joking? He practically blew my head off! I don't know how I'm going to get up the courage to go down to his office again and turn in my column. Maybe I should just quit now—I don't seem to have been too successful as Aunt Fanny."

"Oh, but you are," Caroline said. "That was why I wrote to Aunt Fanny, because I looked at her answers and I thought, this person really cares. She's giving answers that really matter."

"Honest?" Chrissy asked, her eyes lighting up with pleasure.

"Everybody in school was talking about you," Caroline said. "They all thought the column was just what the *Clarion* needed. So don't drop it, please."

Chrissy shrugged her shoulders. "Maybe I'll just hire a bodyguard to escort me to Jay's office, or leave the stuff at his locker. But believe me, I've learned my lesson. From now on I just write impersonal answers. No more getting involved with my clients. It's too uncomfortable being caught in the middle. You should have seen me, running between you and Jay, making sure you both didn't leave, having him blowing in my ear..."

Caroline started to laugh. "Oh, Chrissy, you have the craziest ideas sometimes," she said. "What did I ever do before you got here?"

Chapter 14

Having made her peace with Caroline, Chrissy felt much better about continuing as Aunt Fanny. She wrote her next column and was rewarded with even more letters pouring in. She also managed to steer clear of Jay, merely exchanging a few polite words with him as she dropped off her finished copy or picked up her mail. When he didn't even bother with his sarcastic comments, Chrissy could tell that he would not forgive her in a hurry. She felt bad about him, but decided that there was nothing she could do, other than stay away.

Meanwhile, her fame was growing around school. When Chrissy walked into math class after lunch one day, she encountered a heated discussion about who Aunt Fanny really was.

"I say it's got to be a teacher!" a boy was shouting. "It's too mature to be a kid."

"What's everyone talking about, Donna?" Chrissy whispered to her neighbor as she found her seat.

"Aunt Fanny," Donna whispered back. "She seems to be the hot topic around school right now."

"Really?" Chrissy asked, feeling her cheeks turning pink.

"Oh, sure," Donna went on. "Russell thinks the column has to be written by a teacher."

"Aunt Fanny a teacher?" Chrissy asked in surprise, trying very hard to keep a straight face.

"Well, sure, it's got to be someone mature and sophisticated, doesn't it?" Marcea Horton joined in.

Chrissy spluttered and turned it into a cough.

"Is something wrong?" Marcea asked.

"Sorry, I swallowed my gum," Chrissy muttered, fighting to stop herself from laughing.

"Of course it's a teacher," the boy next to Russell agreed.

"Be serious, Neil. How does Aunt Fanny always seem to know how kids feel?" the girl who sat in front of Chrissy countered.

"A young teacher?" Neil suggested.

"How many teachers are there in this school who are not almost ready for Social Security?" Marcea said cuttingly.

Chrissy tried to hide the smile that ached to creep across her face.

"Why don't you think an ordinary student could write it?" she couldn't resist asking. She was normally pretty quiet in math class, because she was always struggling to understand what the teacher was saying, and had no extra energy for chitchat or wisecracks. Donna Mills, sitting in front of her turned to look at her as if she had spoken without getting permission.

"It can't just be an ordinary student," Donna said witheringly to Chrissy. "They are smart answers, aren't they? Have you actually seen the Aunt Fanny column? It's really witty sometimes."

"Of course I have," Chrissy said, "And I think the answers are pretty good myself, but I still think a student could have written it."

"Maybe a senior who's a whiz in psychology," Donna said.

"And in English. The column is well written, not like the usual trash that shows up in the newspaper!" Donna agreed.

"I think Aunt Fanny should think of going professional," another boy joined in. "Give Ann Landers some competition."

Chrissy looked down to get her math book from her bag. *How about that?* she thought. *They think I'm either a teacher or a psychologist or a great writer, or maybe all three! Not bad at all for somebody who has been here only a few months! I'd love to see their faces if I announced right now it was me.*

When she had a private moment at home,

Chrissy read through her next batch of letters and found that several of them were fan mail, telling her what a good job she was doing, how smart she was, and how much she had helped them. She began to feel a warm glow of satisfaction that she was truly achieving what she had hoped for. One of her fan letters even told her she was a truly great writer.

Maybe I should become a writer, she thought, as she basked in the glory of all the praise. *Maybe I can take over when Ann Landers retires and people all over the country will follow my advice.*

After that Chrissy started studying the professional advice columns in the daily newspaper, noting how each columnist gave the answers her own particular style.

What I need is a little humor, she decided. *Some of these answers are really witty, and some are so dreary that they need livening up! Now that I have a real following that reads my column regularly, I must make sure the standard is high enough.*

"Are you being Aunt Fanny, or can I talk?" Caroline asked as she pushed open the bedroom door later that evening.

"I'm being Aunt Fanny, but you can talk if you want to. It's your room," Chrissy said, looking up from her pile of letters.

"Wow! Are those all letters to you?" Caroline asked in amazement.

"That's right. Aunt Fanny's work is never done."

"I can't get over it. All those people with problems! We must truly be a cuckoo school."

"They are not all problems. Some are just to tell me how wonderful I am," Chrissy said with a grin.

"But even so," Caroline said, eyeing the large pile, "how do you know what to say to all those people? I mean, you're not an expert."

"I'm rapidly becoming one," Chrissy said. "They say practice makes perfect, don't they? Besides, my good old-fashioned Iowa common sense makes me a natural expert. My Grandma Madden always gives the best advice—and I've obviously inherited the talent from her!"

"So you think your advice-giving ability comes from the Madden side of the family? That means I haven't inherited it?"

"Maybe you have," Chrissy said, "but you lack the simple farm girl background, not to mention my big mouth!"

Caroline laughed. "I'd better leave you in peace," she said, "or you might tell the guy who thinks he's a chicken to go see Colonel Sanders!"

"Hey! That's a good line. I bet I could use that sometime," Chrissy said. "I'm trying to give my column some style. It was a little blah, don't you think?"

The smile faded from Caroline's face. "I liked it the way it was, Chrissy. Don't go changing too much, okay?"

"I'm not really changing anything," Chrissy said. "I'm just practicing for the future, when I take over for Ann Landers and Dear Abby combined."

She picked up her pencil and went back to work.

Some of these people need shaking up, she thought after she had read through several more letters. *They all dream of changing their lives, but they don't dare. Maybe a good shaking-up letter will do it for them!*

She began to scribble and by late that night she had finished the whole pile. "More words of wisdom flow from the pen of Aunt Fanny!" she announced to Caroline, waving the finished letters.

Chrissy dropped the letters off with Jay, the next morning, hardly saying a word to him as she did so, then went to classes and waited for her next batch of fan mail. *I bet the kids will love the answer I've given to the girl whose boyfriend is sports-mad*, she thought with a smile as she walked into the apartment that afternoon. *And that girl who has the secret dream—I wonder what it is. Perhaps it's meeting a special boy, like Cara wanted to do, and perhaps she'll dare to do it, after what I've told her. It's great having people asking for my advice. I felt like an outsider here before, but now I know I'm important! I think I'll write and tell Ben about my triumph as Aunt Fanny. I know he'll get a kick out of it!*

She dropped everything on her bed in her room and pulled out her writing paper. Sitting down at her desk, she began to write to him. At first the letter flowed easily as she described her job as Aunt Fanny, leaving out her mixup with Jay and Cara, of course. But then, as she paused, chewing on her pen for inspiration, she began thinking about Ben. What was he doing right now? Was he missing her as much as she was missing him? Then another thought struck her. Was she really missing him? When she had first arrived in San Francisco, she fell asleep each night hugging his picture. Now she hardly even looked at his photograph anymore. Even that awful, hollow feeling in her stomach no longer appeared when she thought of him. She still talked about her boyfriend back home and how terrible it was to be far away from him, but now she asked herself if she really did miss Ben, or if she just missed having a boyfriend around all the time.

She picked up his photo and stared at it, taking in every detail. "Oh, Ben, I do miss you. I really do," she said out loud. "It will be great when I'm back home again and we're together and we can drive around in your old truck and you'll kiss me out on the porch. . . ."

She closed her eyes, trying to conjure up his face in her memory, but it was only a blurred vision of blond hair flopping across his forehead and bright blue eyes—the face from the photo reproduced in her brain, Ben earnestly looking at the camera with those little frown lines around his eyes. He was a serious person by nature, she thought. Not like Jay, who felt life was one huge joke!

Chrissy still felt hot all over when she thought of that evening. *I bet Jay never forgives me for hurting his pride*, she thought. *But he was kind of dumb, too. Imagine him thinking that I was interested in him! He should have gotten the message loud and clear that he was not my type of guy. I like them sincere and dependable, like good old Ben. I'm not one of these slick city types—and I never will be!*

She finished up her letter to Ben, then wrote to her folks, telling them the same things. She could imagine her mother reading the letter out loud around the dining table while her brothers roared their heads off with laughter. It was a good thing they were far away, because they would never be able to take Aunt Fanny seriously, the way she did. They would think it was the funniest thing in the world that people were dumb enough to write to her for advice. They wouldn't stop teasing her about it, day or night.

They just wouldn't believe that I'm a pretty important person, she thought, smiling fondly as she pictured the dining table scene. *To them I'll always be just good old Chrissy who does dumb things sometimes.*

When the *Clarion* came out the following Monday, Chrissy hurried to school full of expectation and secretly anticipating her visit to Jay to see if any new fan letters had arrived. Instead, she met a whispering, nervous knot of girls, including several of her friends, huddled together in the front hall.

"What's up?" she asked them.

They looked up with worried faces. "Oh, hi, Chrissy. I guess you haven't heard the news yet."

"About Lana Wilson?" Maria prompted.

"She probably doesn't even know Lana," Tracy reminded the group. "Do you know who we mean? The little mousy one who doesn't say a word in English class? She sits right behind you."

"Oh, yes, I think I know," Chrissy replied. "What about her?"

"She's run away," Maria blurted out, sounding half scared, half excited. "She left this note for her parents saying she's always dreamed of being a movie star and she never dared tell anyone about it, but now she has the courage to go follow her dream—so she's up and gone to L.A."

Chrissy felt as if she had just stepped into an open elevator shaft. She remembered the letter very clearly—the secret dream nobody knew about. She also remembered her advice to "Go for it, because tomorrow may be too late!" Well, little mousy Lana Wilson had followed her advice to the letter. She had gone for it. All the way to Los Angeles. Chrissy looked from one face to the next.

"I hope they find her," Tracy said. "Can you imagine anybody less likely to survive in L.A. than Lana?"

"She'll probably get picked up at the bus

station by some porno filmmaker or pimp," another girl suggested. "You know how naïve Lana is. She'd believe anything!"

Chrissy turned away and started to run down the hall.

"Hey! Chrissy, what's the hurry?" someone called after her.

"Leave her alone. She's sensitive about things like this," she heard Tracy's voice echoing after her.

Chrissy didn't stop running until she reached the girls' bathroom. She pushed open the door and stood leaning against the cool tile of the wall.

It's all my fault, she kept chanting to herself, over and over. *A girl has run away, all because of me. Just because I was trying to be Ann Landers instead of Chrissy Madden. I have no experience, no right to advise other people. I thought Jay was conceited, but I was really the conceited one!*

She swallowed back the tears that were threatening to cascade out at any moment as she saw the bathroom door open. *There's nothing I can do to help Lana right now*, she thought bleakly, *but I'm going right down to Jay this lunch hour and tell him that I quit. From now on there will be no more Aunt Fanny.*

Chapter 15

Chrissy suffered through her guilt all morning. She tried to concentrate on classes, but pictures of all the terrible things that might be happening to Lana Wilson kept creeping into her mind. Scared as she was for Lana, she also couldn't help being scared for herself. What if there was a big investigation and it was revealed that Chrissy had been the one who caused her to run away? What if they sued her for giving advice without a license? Chrissy felt clammy all over, as if the room was too warm, but in reality it was cold and drafty.

The moment the lunch bell rang, Chrissy headed down the stairs. Jay had never thought much of her column anyway. He'd probably be glad she wanted to quit. He probably wanted her out of his hair after what she did. Even though she gave herself constant pep talks all the way down the basement corridor, she still hesitated outside the office door.

Will you go on in and get it all over with? she told herself fiercely. *This isn't like you! Chrissy Madden is not a scaredy cat. Besides, you don't want Jay Kramer to think you are scared to face him, do you?*

She rapped on the door. There was no answer. She tried the door and found herself looking into an empty room.

"Oh, phooey!" she said out loud. "Now I'll just have to stick around and wait for him."

She walked across the office and perched on the edge of the desk. Minutes passed. The hall outside was totally silent.

"I wish he'd hurry up," she muttered, shivering. "I want to get this over with."

A few more minutes passed. "If he doesn't show up in five minutes, I'm leaving," she said out loud. It seemed to give her confidence to hear her own voice. "What am I worrying about? I'm not scared of him. I'll just say to him, 'Jay Kramer, you don't scare me!'"

"Is that a fact?" a voice asked, about two inches from her left ear.

Chrissy almost fell off the desk in fright. She spun around, scattering papers everywhere. Jay was standing behind her, grinning from ear to ear.

"Holy cow! Where did you pop up from?" she demanded. "You nearly made my heart stop!"

"I was in the closet," Jay said, not taking his eyes off her face for one moment. "I was looking something up in the encyclopedia. Tell me, do you often talk to yourself?"

"Only when I'm the most intelligent person in the room," Chrissy said, her fighting spirit making a rapid recovery from the shock.

"I should have stayed hidden longer. Maybe you'd have said some interesting things," Jay said.

"Didn't your mommy tell you it's very rude to listen in on other people's conversations?" she asked.

"She said it was okay unless there were two or more people talking. One person counts as a nut case, and you are allowed to listen to them."

"You've obviously done a lot of that in your life."

"Done what?"

"Listened to nut cases—otherwise, you'd never have thought you were so hot."

The smile evaporated from Jay's face. "What did you come down here for, anyway? Expecting more fan mail?"

"I came to tell you I am quitting," Chrissy said.

Jay's eyes narrowed. "Quitting the column? why?"

"Because I don't want to do it anymore."

"But you're the most popular thing in the newspaper right now," Jay blurted out. Then he winced. "I never thought I'd hear myself say that, but it's true. You can't just walk out right now. A lot of people have come to rely on you."

"That's why I'm quitting," Chrissy said, toying with the papers on the desk. "I don't want anybody to rely on me. I'm not an expert. I can't advise people."

"But you were doing great. Everybody liked your advice."

"Too much," Chrissy said. "I guess you didn't hear about Lana Wilson yet?"

"Who's she?"

"The type of girl you wouldn't notice. Nobody noticed her, but apparently she dreamed of being a movie star. I advised her to go after her secret dream and she ran away to Hollywood. I feel so terrible."

"But it wasn't your fault. You haven't done anything wrong," Jay said, gently now. "Anyone would have given her the same advice—don't keep dreaming about it, do it. That was the right thing to say. You couldn't have know she'd do something so wild."

"But what if something happens to her? I am the one who told her to do it."

"What about real advice columnists?" Jay asked. "I bet they often give advice which doesn't turn out to be good. They probably tell the wrong women to leave their husbands and send the wrong people to psychiatrists and they never now what harm they've done. You can never predict how people will react to advice. Like I can't predict right now what will happen when I ask you to stay on. . . ."

Chrissy raised her eyes to look at him. Then

she shook her head. "I'm flattered that you finally think my answers are worth something," she said, "but I can't risk another disaster because of my advice. I think I'll leave my newspaper career before it goes downhill any further."

She slid off the desk. " 'Bye, Jay," she said. "I'm sorry we didn't get along better. I guess that was my fault. I'm not the kind of girl to flutter her eyelashes and feed a guy's ego."

She started to walk toward the door.

"Chrissy?" he called out after her.

She turned back.

"Is there anything I can say to make you change your mind?"

She smiled and shook her head. "I don't think so, Jay."

"Chrissy?" He was looking at her, strangely serious. "Even if I told you I was crazy about you and I really want you around?"

"You what?"

"I'm crazy about you, Chrissy."

"Don't tease about things like that."

"I'm not teasing," he said. "I think I fell in love with you the first time you walked into my office, but I didn't realize how I felt about you until I danced with you that night. For a while there I was so happy. I realized I was in love with you and I thought you felt something for me. When you told me the truth it was like getting a slap in the face."

Chrissy looked at him steadily. "You didn't act like you were in love with me," she said. "You acted like I was another helpless female to add to your list of conquests."

Jay turned away from her. "I . . . I talk big sometimes. I've built up this image of myself—Jay Kramer, irresistible to women, smooth talker, doesn't take anything seriously. I guess I created this other person because I'm scared to take things seriously. If I stop laughing for a moment, things hurt too much."

"What sort of things?" Chrissy asked gently.

"Parents who divorce and then fight over me. The first girl I really fall in love with ditches me for a Porsche—I could give you a long list. The last item on it is a girl who invites me to a dance. . . ."

"I'm sorry, Jay. I really thought I was doing a favor for you and Caroline. I had no idea."

"It's okay. How were you to know? You thought I was one of your biggest enemies. We always seemed to fight a lot."

"I enjoyed our fights."

He managed to smile. "So did I. Chrissy?" he asked hopefully. "There's no chance that you and I could. . . . ?"

Chrissy shook her head. "I don't think so, Jay. You're a nice guy but I have a boyfriend back home."

"So there's nothing I can do to make you fall in love with me?" he asked, with a little-boy smile that touched her heart. "I'd try anything once, you know? You want me to rope some cattle or round up some hogs or any other farmy things?"

Chrissy laughed at his joke, then became serious again. "Jay, you can't make a person fall in love with another person. I've learned that much from being Aunt Fanny. Love just happens or it doesn't."

"So you won't even go on a date with me?"

"I don't think that would be a good idea, Jay. You'd keep hoping and trying to make me change my mind, and I'd feel pressured or guilty or both. I don't think we'd enjoy the evening."

"I guess not. Dumb idea." There was a long pause, during which Chrissy curled and uncurled her toes inside her boots and wondered if she should leave. As she turned to go, Jay said, "It's going to seem awful quiet around here without you. Trevor always agrees with everything I say."

"Maybe you should get out more and enjoy the healthy fresh air!" Chrissy suggested.

"Ugh! That's the sort of thing Aunt Fanny would tell me to do!"

"Well, that's the only way you are going to meet more people—down here you're liable to turn into Frankenstein."

"Maybe I already am Frankenstein," he said. "I seem to have a way of screwing things up."

"That's because your outside image doesn't match the person inside," Chrissy said. "I tried that and I know it doesn't work."

"Why do you always have to sound like Aunt Fanny?" he demanded grouchily. "And why are you always right?"

"Just born lucky, I guess," Chrissy said, opening

the door. " 'Bye, Jay. See ya around."

Then she hurried down the hall without looking back.

Chapter 16

That afternoon Chrissy didn't go straight home. A strong wild was blowing off the water, rattling the remaining leaves on their branches and tossing old damp newspapers into the air. Chrissy felt that her mind was full to bursting and somehow she had to sort things out before she got home. It was the right sort of day for walking, anyway. The wind blew at her back and propelled her forward with giant strides, so that before she realized it, she was heading down the hill toward the bay. As she walked past the trendy boutiques with their outlandish clothes and expensive pottery, past the tourist shops with their cheap plastic models of the Golden Gate Bridge and racks of postcards, Chrissy thought for the umpteenth time since she'd arrived here a few months ago how different San Francisco was from the quiet, wide-open fields back home.

Why is life so complicated? she asked herself. *Now I know just how Pandora must have felt when she opened that box and all the troubles of the world came pouring out. Back home nothing bad seemed to happen. I didn't really have any worries. I went to school. School was pretty easy. I practiced for cheerleading squad. I came home. Ben was usually there. We went for drives or to parties. That was life. I mean, sure, we got into trouble sometimes, but never anything like this.* Her mind wandered to her house in Iowa—to the picket fence and her mother's flowers and the shady porch and the family sitting around the dinner table. She saw Ben standing next to his old, red truck, grinning as she ran down the steps toward him. Then his face was replaced with Jay's, smiling his little-boy smile as he looked at her with pleading eyes.

I never realized before that I had the power to cause other people so much pain, she thought. *It's frightening. I wish I was back home again.*

The trouble was that there was no solution. In the past, when Chrissy had felt worried or confused or when she had a decision to make, she had taken a long walk with Bonnie and poured out her problems to the understanding dog. And by the time she got home again, her mind was clear. Now, as she pushed past tourists munching on crab cocktails and pretzels and cotton candy, she looked at them with resentment. Why were they so carefree, with no guilt to weigh down their shoulders?

I tried to help, she thought angrily. *That's the worst part. I really tried to help . . . I wanted to give good advice, and I wanted to get Jay and Caroline together, but now look where it's got me.*

She paused, watching the fishing boats straining at their moorings, hearing the creak of rope and the screeching of sea gulls. *If I could just get on a boat and sail away forever,* she thought wistfully. Then a voice stirred inside her head. *Were you really only trying to help?* the voice asked. *Didn't this Aunt Fanny success go to your head? Didn't you think you were hot stuff as Aunt Fanny? You thought people would be impressed with your clever answers. Wasn't it one of your "clever" answers that made a girl run away? And Jay—weren't you also responsible for giving Jay the wrong idea of how you felt about him? You did act like you were interested so that he would come to the dance. And you did beg him to dance with you so that you could keep him there until Caroline came into the gym.*

Chrissy felt herself go hot and clammy with shame. *I used people,* she thought unhappily. *I did something I always despised. I criticized Jay for his slick answers and for not caring, but I was just as bad.*

She heard Grandma Madden's voice in her mind, giving one of her famous advice handouts. *No good ever comes of not staying true to yourself.*

She's right, Chrissy admitted. *The only reason kids liked the column was because I gave the sort of plain simple answers people would give back home. I didn't try to be a slick city girl. They saw my answers were sincere. Then I got a bad case of a swelled head, and there's nothing I can do to make anything right. I just hope nobody else does anything dumb because of my advice. I'd best go on home and start acting like a normal, plain ordinary person again, and mind my own business.*

She started to walk back up the hill toward Caroline's apartment. She hadn't realized how far she had walked or how fast until she tried to drag her feet up the last flight of steps. Suddenly every muscle in her body seemed to have gone on strike at the same time. She pushed open the front door and collapsed, panting, into the hallway.

Some afternoons Caroline or her mother made hot tea or soup for a snack But this afternoon, when Chrissy was really looking forward to sipping something hot and comforting, she could see the empty kitchen from the hallway. No sign of Caroline or her mother.

"Rats!" she muttered. "Nobody's ever around when you need them! I bet Caroline's out somewhere with the gang."

She dragged her bookbag wearily down the hall and pushed open her bedroom door. She jumped back in alarm as she saw a figure bending over her desk. The figure spun around guiltily, revealing itself to be only Caroline.

"Er . . . Chrissy, you're home," she said, her

eyes darting around suspiciously.

"Caroline, what were you doing at my desk?" she asked.

"Oh, Chrissy, I'm so sorry," Caroline said. "You see, I only meant to help. It was looking so icky, you see, and I knew you didn't have much time these days. . . ."

"What are you talking about?" Chrissy demanded, her nerves already close to the breaking point.

Caroline gave a big sigh and gestured toward the desk. "Elvis," she said. "I think I've killed him."

"You've *what?*" Chrissy rushed toward the goldfish bowl. Elvis was no longer a rich golden color. He was totally white and was feebly swimming backward around his bowl.

"What happened?" Chrissy demanded.

Caroline hesitated, then said, "I thought you were letting his water get all green and disgusting, and I knew you were busy being Aunt Fanny all the time, so I thought I'd help out and change his water for you—but he went all funny right away. What's wrong with him, Chrissy? Is he going to die?"

"Oh Cara," Chrissy said as she stared into the bowl. "You didn't put in water straight out of the faucet, did you?"

"Well, yes. I wanted clean water for him."

"But it's full of chemicals," Chrissy explained impatiently. "You have to let tap water stand for twenty-four hours to let the chemicals evaporate."

"Well, I'm sorry. I didn't know that."

Chrissy couldn't contain herself any longer. She knew inside that Cara had meant well, but after everything that had happened that day, she had to release her tension on someone. "And you accused *me* of interfering with your life!" she yelled. "Who is interfering now, I'd like to know? At least I never killed your goldfish!"

"I didn't mean to kill him, Chrissy. I wanted to help, that's all. I wanted to make it up to you because I blew my top. I don't want Elvis to die. What can we do, Chrissy? I can't bear to see him suffering like this!"

"Where can we find water without chlorine in it?" Chrissy asked, not really expecting an answer.

"It's been raining—maybe there's some rainwater down in the backyard," Caroline suggested hopefully. "I'll go see. . . ."

A few minutes later she came bounding up the stairs. "Chrissy, there was some in the water in the birdbath—not much, but I've got it in this can. Do you think this will be any better?"

"We can try, I guess," Chrissy said, "although the shock of moving him again will probably finish him off. Let's scoop out as much of his water as possible and replace it with the water from the can."

"I'll get a soup ladle from the kitchen," Caroline offered, rushing off again.

Gradually they changed over the water until

Elvis was floating in two inches of rainwater, but now his condition seemed to be even worse.

"We need something to revive him," Chrissy said.

"Some worms?" Caroline suggested. "A lady goldfish to give him a reason to live?"

"We could try artificial respiration," Chrissy said. "Maybe he needs more oxygen."

"How do you propose to do artificial respiration on a goldfish?" Caroline asked. "If you try mouth-to-mouth you're liable to swallow him by mistake."

Chrissy gave Caroline a withering look. "We can try blowing air into his water with straws," she said. Caroline immediately rushed back into the kitchen and returned holding two straws. "Okay. Now blow gently," Chrissy instructed.

For a few moments there was no sound except the gentle gurgling of the bubbles through the water. Suddenly Caroline spluttered.

"Oh, Chrissy!" she said, bursting out laughing. "This is so ridiculous! Artificially respirating a goldfish!"

Chrissy scowled at her and went on blowing. Then suddenly she, too, spluttered and had to come up for air. "I guess it is," she admitted. "Well, we've done all we can for Elvis. I don't hold out much hope, personally." She sank onto her bed with a big sigh. "This definitely ranks as one of the worst days in my life," she said. "I don't know what else could go wrong!"

"You did hear the news about Lana, then?"

Caroline asked. "Somehow I knew it must have been Aunt Fanny's advice that set her to L.A., and I knew it would have upset you. I looked for you after school but I couldn't find you, so I hurried home and you weren't here. I began imagining that you'd run off to Los Angeles to find her yourself!"

Chrissy managed a smile. "I only have three dollars and fifty cents to my name at the moment. I would really have had to *run* all the way."

"I'm glad you're taking it okay," Caroline said, as she sat down at her own desk. "I know how much being Aunt Fanny means to you—how concerned you are about the people who write to you."

Chrissy looked down and stared hard at a wrinkle in her bedspread. If she looked at it in a certain way, it looked like the outline of a fish. "I've quit being Aunt Fanny," she said. "No more trying to butt into other people's lives."

"But you were good at it, Chrissy!"

"What do I know to give advice?" Chrissy said. "I can't even keep my own life straight."

"I thought all your advice was good," Caroline replied. "That's why I wrote to you. I think you should keep on being Aunt Fanny."

Chrissy shook her head. "I'd worry too much, Cara," she said. "Besides, I think it's a good idea for me to stay away from Jay for a while."

"Is he still mad at you?"

Chrissy laughed and shook her head at the same time. "Don't tell a soul about this, but he's kind of . . . fallen for me in a big way."

"You're kidding! Jay Kramer has a crush on you?"

"I'm not that bad, you know," Chrissy said, pretending to be insulted. Some guys find me attractive. Some guys even find me irresistible!" She batted her eyes flirtatiously.

Caroline laughed. "I didn't mean that, and you know it. It's just that I got the impression you and Jay didn't get along."

"So did I," Chrissy admitted, "But he says he enjoyed our little fights. And when I invited him to the dance, he thought I secretly liked him, too. Dumb, huh? My life suddenly seems so complicated."

"So what are you going to do about him? Did you tell him about Ben and smooth things over?" Caroline asked.

Chrissy looked up steadily. "It wasn't as easy as that," she said. "He's really in love with me, Cara. It feels so bad when you know you're hurting another person and you don't want to. He asked me what he could do to make me love him back."

"And what did you say?"

"I realized there was *nothing* he could do. You can't make somebody love you. Either the sparks fly when you meet someone or they don't. I kind of like Jay. At least he's fun, but there's no way I can fall in love with him."

Caroline was silent for a moment, and Chrissy wondered what she was thinking. Finally Caroline asked, "So you think that the sparks have to fly right away or not at all?"

Chrissy nodded.

Caroline sighed, then said, "Then there's no hope for me, is there?"

"With the boy you like?" Chrissy asked.

"Uh-huh. He still doesn't know I like him. I guess he can't like me, or the sparks would be flying."

Caroline looked so sad and helpless, sitting with her chin sunk into her hands, that Chrissy got up and rested her hand on her cousin's shoulder. "Maybe it doesn't have to be love each time, Cara. Maybe you could start out as friends. Have you gotten to know him at all yet?"

Caroline gave a big sigh. "I don't know how to start, Chrissy. I sit there every day in biology class and I don't dare look in his direction because I start blushing. Isn't that dumb? And I'm scared to speak to him, because my jaws don't seem to move properly when he's around. What can I do?"

"You told me to stay out of your life," Chrissy said. "You said you didn't want my help, and I've come to the conclusion you were right."

"But, Chrissy," Caroline pleaded, "I need advice. You can talk to boys. Tell me what to say. I don't need to be set up on a date or anything crazy like that. I just need to know how to get started."

Chrissy shook her head firmly. "How can I tell you what to do? I can only tell you what I'd do, and I'm not you. He's either going to like you for yourself or not at all. You don't want him to become interested in an imitation Chrissy Madden."

"I guess not," Caroline said. "I'll just resign myself to never having another boyfriend. I'll take up crocheting and I'll start breeding Persian cats and doing good deeds, and when I come to Iowa to visit your six kids, I'll be poor old spinster Aunt Caroline!"

Chrissy laughed. "You're crazy!" she said. "You are so smart and you are very pretty. There are going to be loads of boys in your future."

"If I ever dare to talk to them."

"So how did you meet Alex? I thought you told me that matchmaking went out of style."

Caroline laughed. "We were working together on the campaign to prevent the old houses from being torn down. I went over to his house to paint some posters. He flicked some paint on my nose by accident and then he came over to wipe it off. . . ." Her voice trailed away and a dreamy look came into her eyes.

"You see?" Chrissy said quickly, trying to bring Caroline back to the present. The last thing she wanted was for Cara to slip back into her stage of pining for Alex. "When you and a boy were having fun together, doing something you were both interested in, you didn't even notice he was a boy you had to impress. You just acted naturally and things went along from there. If you really like this guy in biology class, just keep waiting. There is sure to be a day when you are dissecting a worm together or something and you'll have enough in common to get talking."

"Maybe," Caroline said with a little sigh. "Unfortunately, we've moved past the worm-dissecting stage. We're on to real animals now and we do it as a group, not as partners. But I will keep on waiting patiently and hoping, Chrissy. Who knows? One day my chance may come. . . ."

Caroline's voice had been becoming softer and softer. Suddenly Chrissy jumped up and uttered a giant yell that almost sent Caroline slithering off her chair. "Holy mazoley! Look at Elvis—he's right side up again!" she shouted excitedly. "Looks like our artificial respiration worked after all. Congratulations, Elvis, sweetheart. Here's some food—eat up! This is terrific. At least one thing seems to be turning out okay. Now, if we could just solve the big problems as easily." Chrissy calmed down and looked at her cousin seriously. "I wish there was something I could do about Lana, and about your secret crush, and about Jay. . . ."

Caroline put an arm around Chrissy's shoulder, and they watched Elvis nibble tentatively at a speck of food. "Some things you can't do anything about, Chrissy," she said gently. "You can only wait and hope that they turn out all right. That's what we have to do right now." Caroline started toward the door. "Come on, I'll make you some chicken soup to celebrate saving Elvis's life."

Chapter 17

Chrissy walked past the biology lab for the fourth time in five minutes. From inside the half-open door came an unfamiliar, unpleasant smell. Chrissy peered in. Classes were over for the day and the place was deserted. Chrissy had hurried over to the lab, telling herself that she would meet Caroline and see if she wanted to walk home together. She would not admit to herself that she was more than a little bit curious about Cara's mysterious boy from biology class.

Rats! I'm too late, she realized as she peered into the empty room. *It's not fair that I have math right over on the other side of the building. Now I'll never get a chance to spy on them. . . .*

She broke off this thought, horrified at the way her mind was working.

*Chrissy Madden, you promised not to interfere!
Leave Caroline to meet her own boy. You won't
be helping her by hanging around spying, and
you know it!*

She glanced up and down the empty hallway.
But it would be nice just to know who he is, she
thought wistfully. *After all my hard work snooping, I'd love to know his name. Maybe there's a
class list lying on the teacher's desk*

And before she could stop to consider the
consequences, she found herself sneaking
through the doorway. Inside, the smell was over-
powering, and a half-dissected object was lying
on a side table. Chrissy skirted around it, trying
not to look. *Poor little animal*, she thought. *I'm
glad I'm not in biology here. If they made me cut
up a poor little mouse or frog, I'd quit.*

The teacher's desk was completely clean of any
papers, but there were notices on the bulletin
boards around the room and Chrissy wandered
around, glancing at them to see if they gave any
clues. The whole lab was so different from anything back home. She had taken biology back in
Danberry, but the course had consisted mainly of
drawing diagrams of the insides of flowers and
watching bad movies on the human reproductive
system. They had not been allowed to cut up
anything other than a snapdragon and an onion.
This lab, however, was full of experiments—glass
jars on shelves held horrible pickled things, and
there was a full-color poster of the insides of a
fetal pig. And at the back of the room, there was

even a cage. Chrissy paused beside it and looked in. Nestled in the straw was a soft, brown rabbit.

Chrissy was crazy about all animals, but she had an extra special attachment to rabbits. She'd had a fuzzy white bunny when she was younger and had trained it so well that it ran free in the house and came when it was called. Now, as she looked at this rabbit, all the memories of home and her own pet came flooding back. Sensing that there was somebody near his cage, the rabbit uncurled and hopped across to the bars, whiffling hopefully at her hand, his whiskers quivering. Caroline's words echoed in Chrissy's head: *We're dissecting real animals now.*

"Is that what they're planning to do?" Chrissy whispered to the rabbit. "Are you next? They're not going to cut you up, are they?"

The soft whiskers quivered in reply against her hand. The thought of the gentle brown bunny lying pinned down on a table with his body sliced open was more than she could bear.

I'm not going to let them do it, she decided. *I'll probably get into terrible trouble, but I don't care.* Carefully she opened the cage door. The rabbit leaned forward hopefully, looking for food Chrissy reached in and grabbed at him, picking him up by the loose skin behind his neck and swinging him out in one movement.

"You're coming with me, Thumper," she said. Then she stuffed him inside her jacket and crept out of the building.

Caroline was not around when Chrissy got

home, but Caroline's father was puttering around in the kitchen fixing himself a snack.

"Must be cold today," he said, smiling at Chrissy as she appeared in the doorway. "You're wearing so many layers, you look like a snowman."

Chrissy smiled back, praying hard that the rabbit wouldn't wriggle while her uncle's eyes were on her jacket.

"It's nice and warm in here," she said, moving away as quickly as she could. "I'm going to get out of all this clothing."

She scurried off to her bedroom and shut the door behind her. Then she lifted the rabbit from her jacket and put it down on the floor. It looked around nervously, then hopped toward her chest of drawers, disappearing underneath its legs. Now that she had the rabbit here, Chrissy fully realized what she had done—she had stolen school property, an act which might be enough to get her suspended and which would surely go on her record. Plus the fact that she had brought home a rabbit she certainly couldn't keep. As if to emphasize that point, she heard her uncle's loud sneeze coming from the kitchen Caroline had said he was allergic to animal fur. The Kirbys probably wouldn't even let her build a hutch for it out on the balcony. It was probably a violation of city building codes or animal laws or something.

And all they'll do at school is just go out and buy themselves a new rabbit tomorrow, she thought unhappily, *and I can't go on rescuing them*!

But even considering all these factors, Chrissy was still glad that she managed to save this rabbit. *If I can find him a good home, then at least I've done one good thing*, she thought. *Caroline will understand—surely she will see that he's sweet and gentle and he shouldn't be killed. . . .*

Caroline did not come home until Chrissy and her aunt and uncle were already seated for dinner. She must have let herself in very quietly, because the first Chrissy knew of her arrival was when the kitchen door opened and Caroline dragged herself to the table. Her volleyball team had played an away from home game, and they had been badly defeated.

"You should have seen those girls," she said as she sank into a chair. "They were gorillas— absolute animals."

As Caroline said the word *animal*, Chrissy happened to look up. Out of the corner of her eye she saw something move past the open kitchen doorway. She watched with horror as the rabbit paused behind her uncle's back and began to sniff at the interesting smells in the kitchen. Suddenly her uncle gave an enormous sneeze that made everyone at the table jump and scare the rabbit back out into the hall again.

"I think I must be coming down with a cold," he said from behind his handkerchief. "My nose has been running all evening."

Chrissy slid from her seat. "I'll get you a box of

tissues," she said, hurrying toward the kitchen door.

"Don't worry about it now, dear, your dinner will get cold," her uncle said.

"Oh, it's okay. I'll be right back," Chrissy said, slipping out into the hall and making a grab for the rabbit.

"She's a sweet kid," she heard her uncle say as she carried the rabbit back to her room. She'd have to tell Caroline as quickly as possible, so that she wouldn't leave the door open again.

I just hope she's not too tired after that game. She might get hysterical before I can explain, Chrissy thought gloomily. *I hope she's got a good idea about someone we can give the rabbit to.*

The moment dinner was over, Caroline got up. "I am beat," she said. "I'm going to soak in a long, hot tub. I bet I'll discover a million bruises!"

Chrissy jumped up, too.

"Chrissy, would you load the dishwasher for me, please?" her aunt asked. "We have to be at the concert in twenty minutes."

"Oh, sure, Aunt Edith, I'll be back in a moment," Chrissy answered, one hand already on the door. She sprinted out of the room and leaped to the bedroom door just as Caroline was about to open it.

"Let me go in first!" she said, panting.

Caroline looked at her as if she had turned into a dangerous lunatic.

"Why? Have you got King Kong in there?"

"Not exactly, and I can explain everything. . . ."

She opened the door cautiously and Caroline followed her into the room. The first thing they both saw was a floor littered with rabbit droppings. Caroline's eyes opened wide. "Mon Dieu! You *have* got King Kong in here!"

"Shh!" Chrissy warned, closing the door hastily. "I don't want your folks to know."

"Okay. What is it?" Caroline asked, looking nervously around the floor. "You are talking to somebody who has no experience with animals. I want to know whether I've got to leap onto a chair in cease it bites my foot. I haven't had my rabies shots, you know."

Chrissy knelt down and began looking under the furniture. Finally she reached under Caroline's bed and pulled out the rabbit.

"It's only this," she said, holding him up.

Caroline's face softened. "Oh, isn't he sweet!" She stepped forward to stroke him. "Where did you get him? You know, we've got one just like him in the lab at school. I always save him a carrot from my lunch."

Chrissy took a deep breath. "This *is* the one from the lab at school," she said.

"Chrissy Madden! Have you gone out of your mind?" Caroline shrieked. "What on earth made you take him?"

"I should have thought that was obvious. I didn't want you butchers to dissect him." She held the rabbit close to her cheek.

"Dissect him? Chrissy, this is Harvey. He's my biology teacher's pet rabbit. He has lived in that lab all year."

"Holy cow!" Chrissy said, sinking with Harvey onto her bed. "How was I to know? You said you dissected all kinds of animals and I saw him, so I thought . . ."

'Yes, but those animals always arrive dead at the lab. We don't have to kill them first—some medical company supplies them all ready for us to use."

"Oh," was all Chrissy could say.

Caroline looked at her suspiciously. "What were you doing in the biology lab? Christina Madden, were you trying to interfere again? Were you trying to set me up with a boy?"

"Of course not. I said I wouldn't do that." She began tickling Harvey behind his ears, not looking up at her cousin.

"Then what were you doing in my biology lab?"

"I only dropped by to see if you were walking home today," Chrissy answered, hoping she sounded casual.

"But you always meet me by my locker," Caroline said. "Let me just tell you that I welcome your advice on speaking to boys, but I do not welcome your meddling. If you tell him about me, I'll never speak, to you again!"

"I wouldn't do that, Cara. I promise," Chrissy said. "Now what are we going to do about Harvey?"

"What are *you* going to do, you mean," Caroline said dryly.

"All right. What am I going to do?"

"Take him back, of course."

"But, Cara—what if somebody sees me?"

"You'd better think up a good explanation."

"Won't you come with me? We could go first thing in the morning and maybe nobody will have noticed he was missing," Chrissy pleaded.

"I don't want to get involved in this," Caroline said. "Bad things always seem to happen to me when I get involved in your dumb schemes."

"But I don't want to get in trouble, especially when I thought I was doing such a good deed. I need you for my cover to get into the biology lab."

Caroline sighed. "We'll see in the morning. The big question is: What are we going to do with Harvey tonight?"

"All he needs is a box with some old newspapers in it," Chrissy said hopefully.

Caroline hesitated. "I suppose he can have the box my stereo came in," she offered. "I wouldn't want him to feel cold or scared." She rummaged inside her closet and pulled out a large box, out of which she tipped snow boots, theater programs, a moose hat, and an assortment of other junk.

Chrissy settled Harvey in his box and later got him some lettuce and alfalfa from the kitchen.

"He's such a good little thing!" Caroline exclaimed, looking down at him with gentle eyes. "I've never had an animal in the house, not since I brought home a guinea pig in kindergarten. My dad sneezed at that, too." She sighed. "It's a shame, really, because I can see it would be really nice to have a furry little animal waiting for me at the end of a hard day. If it weren't for my dad's allergy, I bet I could convince my folks. After all, he's so good. He's no trouble, is he?"

Caroline squatted beside the rabbit, petting him as he crunched his dinner noisily. By the time the girls got into bed, Harvey was already asleep, curled into a little brown ball. Chrissy looked down at him fondly as she closed her own eyes.

When she opened them again, she was conscious of light shining into them *It can't be morning already*, she thought. Then she noticed that the light was coming from the doorway. The door was open a few inches and a thin streak of light was falling right on her face. *Someone's left the door open*, she thought drowsily. Then she sat upright. *The door open? I hope Harvey didn't . . .* She peered down into the box. It was empty.

"Holy mazoley!" she muttered, leaping out of bed to shut the door before searching frantically around the room. When she was satisfied that Harvey was not there, she tiptoed over to Caroline's bed.

"Caroline, wake up!" she whispered, bending over her cousin's sleeping body.

"What is it?" Caroline mumbled. "Let me sleep."

"Harvey's gone!"

"What?"

"The rabbit. The rabbit got out. Somebody opened the door!"

"Oh." Caroline's eyes opened and focused on her cousin. "That must have been me. I went to get a drink of water I thought I closed the door all the way, but you know how it doesn't catch sometimes."

"Well, Harvey took full advantage. You soon learn with animals that they can slip through a crack you wouldn't have thought a hair could get through, let alone a hare!"

"Most amusing." Caroline sat up, fully awake now. "I suppose you want me to help you find him?"

"He can't have gone far," Chrissy said hopefully "unless somebody left a window open."

"My parents always sleep with their window open," Caroline said, jumping out of bed. "You don't think he'd leap out through a third-story window, do you?"

"I hope not," Chrissy replied. "Most likely he went for the kitchen. You take the living room and I'll do the kitchen."

A search of both places produced no sign of Harvey. Neither did a search of the bathroom.

"That can only mean one thing," Chrissy said gloomily. "He went into your parents' room!"

A loud sneeze and a groan came from the half-open door of the Kirbys' bedroom. Caroline nodded grimly. "That sounds like Harvey, all right. Come on—let's try and get him."

"Why don't you try?" Chrissy suggested. "I'd

feel kind of silly if your parents woke up and saw me."

"You should have thought of that before you stole Harvey," Caroline said firmly. "I am not catching a rabbit single-handed. You're the animal expert—you do it. Now get in there."

Chrissy heaved a big sigh as she followed Caroline. Inside the door the half light showed two peacefully sleeping figures, an open window, and nothing moving. The girls looked at the window and then exchanged a worried glance.

"Can rabbits jump that high?" Caroline mouthed.

"I don't think so," Chrissy mouthed back. She got down on her hands and knees and began groping under pieces of furniture. Caroline's father sneezed again—even louder this time—and Chrissy jumped so violently that she hit her head on the bottom of the desk. Both girls froze as he mumbled something and turned over.

"He's not here," Caroline whispered.

"Try under the bed," Chrissy suggested.

"There's not enough room," Caroline whispered back.

"You don't know rabbits," Chrissy said. She lay on the floor and stretched her arm out as far as she could. "I can't reach far enough," she whispered. "Go around the other side."

Caroline went reluctantly. She lay on the other side and stretched out her own arm. "He's not . . . Eek!"

"Shh!" Chrissy warned. The two sleepers

moved restlessly, a sign that they were coming out of deep sleep and dangerously near full consciousness. Chrissy peered under the bed, but it was too dark to see.

"I think I touched something," Caroline whispered. "Over here, by the leg."

As Chrissy reached toward the leg of the bed, her hand brushed against something soft and warm. "Here Harvey," she whispered. She tried to close her hand around him, but he shot off in Caroline's direction. "He's coming—" Her instruction was cut off by Caroline's horrified gasp.

"Grab him!' Chrissy instructed.

"You grab him. He's under my armpit and he's rapidly trying to burrow into my body, and my other arm's trapped under the bed."

Chrissy started giggling as she pulled the rabbit out from his hiding place. She giggled even more as they tiptoed out of the room.

"Mama mia! Am I glad we've limited you to a goldfish!" Caroline said, sinking back onto her bed with a sigh. "I couldn't take this much excitement on a daily basis."

"But wasn't that fun?" Chrissy asked. "I had to keep holding my breath so I didn't burst out laughing."

"Oh, it was a barrel of laughs," Caroline said, pulling the covers up over her. "I'm cold, I'm covered in dust, my heart nearly stopped beating when Harvey tried to burrow into my armpit, and I've lost the best part of my night's sleep."

"So you will help me take him back in the

morning, won't you?" Chrissy asked in a small voice.

"Anything but go through another night like this!" Caroline said. "I'll say one thing for you, Chrissy—life certainly isn't dull with you around. To think that before you came, I went quietly to sleep every night, worn out by an uneventful day at school and a peaceful evening doing my homework."

"Sounds boring," Chrissy muttered as she stroked Harvey in his box, next to her bed.

"You're right." Caroline's muffled voice came from under her covers. "Now that you mention it—it was! Good night."

"Good night, Cara. Good night, Harvey." There was a pause, and then: "Oh, sorry, I almost forgot. Good night, Elvis."

Chapter 18

"So far, so good," Caroline whispered as they turned the corner into the science wing. "As long as Mr. Hayley is not there early today, we'll be fine."

"Do you think he's the understanding type, if he is there early?" Chrissy asked. "Anyone who keeps a rabbit as a pet can't be all bad."

"He's got a quick temper," Caroline said, "and, frankly, I'd rather not be on the wrong side of him. I'd like an A in his class."

"We'd better hurry up," Chrissy muttered. "Harvey is getting restless. It doesn't feel too great to have an impatient rabbit running around inside your jacket. They have claws, you know."

"Okay. Let's make a run for it," Caroline whispered. She started to sprint up the hallway and paused by the biology lab door. "It's fine. We're in luck," she called. "The room's open and nobody's here yet!"

Chrissy followed her cousin to the back of the room. "I bet nobody even noticed that he was missing," she said in a normal voice. "What a piece of luck. Here, Harvey, you can come out now. You get to go home." She opened the cage and began to remove Harvey from her jacket. She was just reaching to put him in the cage when there was the sound of movement behind her. Chrissy spun around to see a large figure coming through the doorway. She knew she had no time to lose as she quickly flung Harvey into the cage. " 'Bye, Cara. I think I'd better be going," she called, running past the figure and into the hallway.

I know that was mean of me, she said to herself as she collected her books at her locker in another hall, safely away from the science wing, *but Harvey is back where he belongs and Cara won't get in trouble for being in her own biology lab. Thank heavens that all turned out just fine. I'm so glad I didn't have to explain why I took the rabbit. I've done some pretty dumb things lately, but that was definitely the last of them. From now on I'm going to be like Cara—mature, sensible, calm, quiet. . . .*

"Chrissy Madden, you rat, I want to talk to you!" Caroline's yell made everyone in the hall turn around. She was running toward Chrissy, who just stared at her cousin's beet red face, and thought for a fleeting moment that she saw smoke coming out of her ears. People backed out of Caroline's way as she grabbed Chrissy by the shoulders.

"Cara? are you mad at me?" Chrissy asked, innocently. Caroline started shaking her. "Have I done something? You didn't get in trouble because of me, did you?"

"You worm! After you promised!" Caroline yelled. "It was all a plot!"

"What are you talking about? Will you let go of my sweater! You're strangling me!" Chrissy yelled back.

"I'd like to, believe me," Caroline said. "To think I didn't suspect anything, when you obviously arranged the whole thing!"

"Cara—heavens to Betsy—what are you talking about?"

Caroline released Chrissy's sweater and stood glaring at her. "Don't pretend that you don't know," she said angrily. "You can't fool me with your Little Miss Innocent act anymore. Those baby-blue eyes belong to a snake. I can't believe I fell for your trick."

"What trick?" Chrissy asked, honestly confused.

"You knew he came in early to feed the animals, didn't you?" Caroline growled. "You knew he'd arrive when we were there and I'd be trapped with him."

"With your teacher?"

"With Jim! Who else?"

Understanding was beginning to dawn for Chrissy. "The boy you like? He's the one who walked in?"

"Don't pretend you didn't know it. You found out he was the teacher's assistant, didn't you? You found out he came in early to feed the animals. I can just see your crazy, warped mind plotting this way: 'Cara will have to help me take the rabbit back, and then they'll meet and have to talk to each other, because she'll have to explain what she was doing with the rabbit cage open before school.' Well, you'll be pleased to know it worked. He did talk to me, and I answered him, stuttering like a complete fool, and I couldn't think of any good excuse for having the rabbit cage open and the rabbit half out of it, so I told him the truth and now he thinks I'm a complete idiot and he'll never talk to me again, so thanks a lot!" The bell sounded loudly above their heads. "I've got to go. Don't bother to wait for me after school, because I'm not speaking to you ever again after this," Caroline said. "At least *I* keep my promises." And she ran off, leaving Chrissy staring open mouthed after her.

Why do things just seem to happen to me? she thought miserably. *How was I to know the boy she likes came in early to feed the animals? I don't even know who he is!*

She sat unhappily through her classes, and avoided Cara and her group at lunchtime. After school she packed her things, flung her book bag onto her back, and set off for home, dragging her feet down the school steps.

Head down, collar turned up against the wind, she started down the hill. She hardly noticed the group of students standing on the corner. As she pushed past them one of them said, "That's her. That's the one who did it."

Chrissy looked up to see Caroline pointing at her calmly. Then she followed Caroline's gaze back to two boys. She didn't know the blond one, but the other one was Jay. As her eyes met Jay's, they both did a double take.

"I might have known," Jay said with an exaggerated sigh. "When Jim told me he had this great story for the newspaper about a girl kidnapping a rabbit, I should have guessed that nobody in the school would be crazy enough to do it except you."

Chrissy looked from one face to the next, feeling hot and embarrassed.

"So you two already know each other?" Jim asked in a surprised voice. "You didn't tell me that, Caroline."

"It didn't seem important," Caroline said, giving Chrissy a sweet smile. "With newshounds, only the news is important, and you must admit, it makes a nice human-interest story."

"So what do you say we go and get a cappuccino and a pastry at the Italian bakery," Jim suggested. "You can do your interviewing while we eat. How's that, Jay?"

"It's okay. I don't think it would make such a good story after all," Jay replied, looking quickly at Chrissy and then away again.

"Then let's just go for the coffee and no interview," Jim said. He glanced hopefully in Caroline's direction.

"Good idea. You two will join us, won't you?" Caroline asked, her cheeks coloring with pleasure as Jim looked at her.

"Will you risk having a cup of coffee with me?" Jay asked Chrissy.

There was something in his eyes, that little-boy insecurity, that made her hesitate. He had tried to smooth things over, to save her from embarrassment, when he could have played up the story to the limit. That was a very un-Jay-like thing to do. She could hardly reject him in front of other people and add to his misery. She'd already hurt him enough.

Chrissy smiled. "It seems as if it's all been arranged for us," she said.

As they began to walk down the hill, Jay fell into step beside Chrissy.

"The office has seemed real quiet the past few days," he said. "It's been so boring down there that I've decided to take your advice and come up for air. You were right. There is a world up here!" He glanced across at her. "You haven't had any second thoughts about coming back, have you?"

"I couldn't, Jay," Chrissy said, firmly shaking her head. "Aunt Fanny was just too much responsibility. You need someone with experience to answer personal letters like these. I was so glad they found Lana Wilson and brought her home safely. I couldn't go through anything else like that."

"So why don't you join the staff of the paper and write other stuff? Your writing is good, you know."

"You're not just saying that to get me back again?" Chrissy asked.

"No, I mean it," Jay replied earnestly. "I think you write well. There are plenty of things you could write besides Aunt Fanny."

"I still have a boyfriend back home, Jay. I don't think you're going to make me change the way I feel about you."

Jay managed a hopeful smile. "Do you think you could learn to be friends?"

Chrissy gave him a long, steady look. "I think I could, but I enjoy being enemies better."

"So we'll be friends who fight a lot. Compromise, okay?"

"Okay," Chrissy said. "I'd like to write for the paper, Jay, and I've missed our fights."

"Great!" he said. "I'm glad that Caroline arranged this."

"Oh—Caroline arranged this, did she?" Chrissy asked.

"I guess so," Jay said. "Maybe she saw that the newspaper needed you and you needed the newspaper. She was just doing a little public service."

"Oh, sure," Chrissy said, eyeing Caroline's back as her cousin turned into the bakery ahead of them. "Caroline's great at public service. Even better than me."

The moment they were in the café, Chrissy dragged Caroline into the ladies' rest room.

"Okay. Start explaining!" she said, giving Caroline a menacing stare. "I seem to remember that your parting words to me were that you would never speak to me again. You changed your mind pretty rapidly, didn't you?"

Caroline grinned triumphantly. "I decided to give you a dose of your own medicine instead. You see, your crazy scheme did work. Apparently, Jim didn't think I was an idiot. I was right in my letter—he was simply waiting for a chance to get to know me. He came past my locker at lunchtime and we started talking. Then we ate lunch together and got along just great. Well, Jim and Jay are pretty good friends—they're in the same lab group in biology. When Jay sat with us at lunch and Jim started telling him about the rabbit, I couldn't resist hinting that it would make a good story for the paper and that he should interview the girl himself. I just failed to mention it was you. So how do you like it when someone else arranges your life?"

"Cara," Chrissy said slowly, "I meant what I said this morning. I did not arrange for you to meet Jim. I had no idea who he was. I'd never seen him before in my life until this afternoon. However strange it may sound, the whole thing was pure coincidence."

There was a long pause. "You wouldn't lie to

your own flesh and blood?"

"Cross my heart and hope to die."

Caroline looked at her, wide-eyed. "Chrissy, I'm sorry. I really thought—well, you know what I thought."

"It's okay. I can understand how it must have looked."

"Are you very mad at me?"

"No." Chrissy turned away and straightened her hair in the mirror. "You know, it's funny, but when I saw it was Jay, I was really glad to see him again. I think I've been missing him."

"So you think you'll see more of him?"

"I might go to work on the paper," Chrissy said. "No Aunt Fanny stuff, just as a regular reporter. So I guess we will be around each other—just as friends."

"Oh, sure," Caroline said. "Just friends, of course."

Chrissy shot her a sideways glance. "And I take it you'll be seeing more of Jim?"

"It seems that way," Caroline said, blushing and grinning at the same time. "It's funny, but when we had something to talk about, I found I could talk to him pretty easily. He keeps rabbits of his own, you know—and hamsters and rats. He's invited me to see them."

"That's a new one—come up and see my rats sometime," Chrissy said, smiling at her cousin. "I'm glad for you, Cara. I'm glad my meddling all worked out in the end."

"I hope my meddling works out for you, too,

Chrissy," Caroline said. "It would be fun to double date, wouldn't it? We could go to the zoo and Marine World. . . ."

"And maybe I could persuade Jay to kiss the killer whale this time," Chrissy said, laughing.

Caroline laughed, too. "I think poor Jay is in for a stormy friendship," she said.

"But he likes it that way," Chrissy explained. "And so do I. I was missing the fights with my brothers—although after the way you yelled at me and grabbed me in the hall today, I think you're beginning to take their place."

Caroline looked guilty. "I'm sorry. I don't know what came over me," she said. "I've never done anything like that before. I was so mad that I'd blown my one chance with Jim. . . ."

Chrissy grinned. "I think my personality is rubbing off on you," she said. "You were quiet and calm until you met me."

"And you've calmed down a lot," Caroline said. "You don't fly off the handle or yell so much anymore. Maybe we are rubbing off on each other."

"Let's hope we pick up the other's good qualities, not the bad," Chrissy said.

"Don't worry," Caroline said firmly. "We are Madden and Kirby—the dynamic duo, the terrific twosome. . . ."

"Super cousins!" Chrissy exclaimed, laughing. Then she loooked back at the door. "Oops! I'd forgotten all about the boys for a minute there," she said, still laughing. "We'd better get back to them or they'll think we've escaped through the back window."

As Chrissy turned to go, Caroline grasped her arm. "Hey! Chrissy, pinch me—I can't believe this is happening. You and me and those two great guys out there. We are going to have the best time!"

"You know, Cara," Chrissy said, "for once in your life I believe you're right!"

Here's a sneak preview of *Nothing in Common*, book number five in the continuing SUGAR & SPICE series from Ivy Books.

"Bad news?" Caroline asked, sitting on the bed beside her cousin.

"Terrible," Chrissy said. "I think I'm losing Ben to Tammy Laudenschlager. He promised to help her build rabbit cages for her 4-H project." She lay back and gave a big, unhappy sigh. "I wonder how much it would cost to fly home for spring break."

"Are you sure it's wise to go rushing back?" Caroline asked. "You might do more harm than good. You might lose your famous temper with Ben and send him right into Tammy's arms."

"I've just got to go home," Chrissy said. "I miss everyone so much. I didn't see my family for Christmas, and now my boyfriend is about to leave me for another girl. I've got to go home, or I'll die."

"Calm down, Chrissy," Caroline said gently. "We'll talk to my parents tonight."

Chrissy leaped up from the bed and flung her arms around Caroline. "You're the greatest, you know that? I wish I could take you along to tell me what to do about Tammy. You're always so cool and sensible, and you don't fly off the handle like me—" She broke off and stared at Caroline. "I've got the greatest idea!" she yelled. "Caroline, you're coming with me!"

ABOUT THE AUTHOR

Janet Quin-Harkin is the author of more than thirty books for young adults, including the best-selling *Ten-Boy Summer* and *On Our Own*, its sequel series. Ms. Quin-Harkin lives just outside of San Francisco with her husband, three teenage daughters, and one son.